CONTENTS

to Denise, for starting a fire
to Marita, for seeing me
to Jen, for unexpected insight
to Suzanne, for believing

seeds

"What a sight."

Cape Johns is deceptively beautiful in the early morning. At least it is from the top of the tower. Disorderly steel industrial parks take on the appearance of dark, ornate palaces, shrouded by the glimmering screen of the river, guarded at the shore by towering four-legged freight cranes. If it's the right time of year, any number of silhouetted flocks will cross the golden skyline, and at no time does the rumble of traffic below overtake the meditative silence of the tower's pinnacle. It's a panorama that many Capers and a lucky few out-of-state students are privy to, and one of these was Dominic Winters.

During what had become a morning ritual, Dom and his sketchbook would make their way to the top of Ferron Tower and transfer scenery directly to paper with nary a creative impulse in between. This period was Dom's most concerted effort to replicate and *not* create, his self-imposed decompression therapy, and it was lately becoming the highlight of his existence.

Less than an hour of morning separates the mirage of dawn from the harsh reality of daylight, when you have to travel a few miles inland to escape the oppressive noise, fumes and outright ugliness of the east end. The serene art school campus is really the only visually agreeable area of Cape Johns, at the same time a symbol of pride and scorn to the blue-collar community surrounding it. Why the forward-leaning school coexists with this town has long been a fiercely-debated topic among local historians, and how they coexist, no one really knows.

✚

Alex had a habit of rubbing his belly at the end of every meal, though there wasn't much of one to rub. From the looks of them, he and Dom might have been brothers — both similarly tall and lanky, both with dishevelled hair (albeit in different colors), and both of them nearly always clad in worn-out, paint-spattered clothes regardless of the occasion. Rarely was one seen without the other unless Karen happened to be around.

Alex pushed what was left of his food aside, burped into his hand and said, "All artists are jealous of good ideas. Goes with the territory. It's the 'why didn't I think of that' syndrome."

Dom wasn't encouraged. "Yeah, I know," he said while fiddling with his receipt absentmindedly, staring down at nothing with a stolid look. "I just feel like there's a wall I can't break, a conceptual threshold. Everything I create is wishy-washy."

Alex cringed and opened his mouth to speak but decided that an objection would be transparently insincere. He conceded the point by pursing his lips. "All right. I guess if I didn't know you so well I'd disagree. Most of us mortals would love to have your portfolio." For Alex, the search for iconic inspiration wasn't a priority; he was a competent but complacent artist who was as happy doing contract work as rendering divine inspiration. Maybe more so, since it required less mental effort.

Dom could never be satisfied with that. Dom knew, partly because he had always been told so and partly because he simply felt it, that he had the potential to become the 21st century's Pablo Picasso. If that feeling wasn't accurate, then it was the cruelest joke fate could have played on any man who considered himself an artist.

He stared vacantly out the window. "I... put so much sweat into the search for a good idea, but I all I get is passable ones. In a way it's not fair that my life has been uneventful — where am I supposed to get inspiration if nothing terrible ever happens?"

Alex pouted, looked longingly at Dom, then quietly said "poor baby" before laughing at himself, resulting in a Dom eye roll. The diner was starting to fill up with undergrads ambling in from late lab classes. "Let's get out of here before I start sobbing in front of the kiddies," Alex said before leaving an art-student-standard 10% tip on the table. They made their way to the door. As they walked back down the alleyway to the grad studio space, Alex spoke up again. "You know, I think the naming thing is blocking your third eye. Maybe if you would settle for 'Untitled' just once..."

"Oh, don't start."

For a moment, Carol Thompson thought those art school shits hadn't left her a tip at all. But no, it was just hiding underneath the bill: $1.75 in quarters. She took a calming breath and internally reminded herself not to judge — she didn't know their situation, and it was fair to guess that they weren't walking around with cash falling out of their wallets, expensive as that art school must be. Too tired to waste energy hating on them, anyway. Her nine hour shift had officially ended, and it was all she could do to ignore her knee pain enough to finish up and get out the door.

She carried the discarded dish stack into the kitchen, tossed her apron in the hamper, washed her hands, and punched out. "I'm outta here, Bill" she called to the cook after gathering her coat and purse.

Bill turned away from the grill and blew her a kiss, which made her chuckle. "Drive safe, Carol."

She walked out the back door into a glossy, post-rain parking lot under a grey sky. She always tried to park her maroon '88 Chevy Nova (a re-badged Toyota Corolla; she had only narrowly avoided the scorn of her "buy American" father while still investing in Japanese reliability) near the street-side back corner of the lot to reduce the likelihood of break-ins, since it was more visible under the streetlight there. The car ran, but it was long in the tooth, and while Carol wasn't a particularly hefty person, this model year's springs weren't particularly long-lasting, so her Nova had a visible leftward lean that was more pronounced when she sat down in it. It also had packing tape across one taillight and wore a faded Bush-Quayle '92 bumper sticker (that she was politically and aesthetically ambivalent about), and a back right fender dent courtesy of an anonymous parking lot asshole.

McMaster Road remained fairly busy until well after dark this time of year, so Carol adopted her special routine for backing into her driveway: pull into the middle "lane" (a diagonal-striped margin between the real lanes) with her left turn signal on — even though there was no left turn — then reverse the car to the right when the traffic subsided, pulling backward into the driveway so that she could pull out safely tomorrow. It wasn't her and Keith's dream location, but it was hard to imagine squeezing into the other options they could afford that sat on less trafficked lots. The situation took some getting used to when they rented it last year, but it worked.

Mrow? "Dammit, Crystal, why are you out here?" she muttered to herself, petting the tortoise shell cat that her boys well knew was supposed to be locked inside hours ago. Carol grunted as she bent down to take the cat under her arm, then walked through the fence gate to a side door featuring the tattered frame of a failed storm door that was bungeed to the adjacent gutter spout with a disemboweled screen hanging down from its lower window.

Denny was doing homework at the kitchen table. Immediately he saw the cat and said, "sorry mama" in a broody voice before she could even complain, then went back to his work. His face was dark and he seemed oddly sad, which took her off guard — she was fully expecting to begin griping at both of them, but refrained when it seemed like something was off. *The Simpsons* was playing in the living room, Edwin laying on the floor and Keith on the couch holding a Michelob.

Keith vaguely noticed movement to his right, then turned and saw his wife. "Hey babe. What's up?"

"Hey," Carol responded, then tilted her head significantly toward her youngest.

"Mm, yeah," Keith said, then waved a come hither gesture with the index finger of his beer hand as he rose from the couch, walking toward their bedroom. Edwin, who would normally have at least said hello, glanced backward briefly but was otherwise quietly glued to the TV.

Carol pulled the door to behind her as Keith, unshaven and wearing an old Patriots t-shirt with khaki shorts, sat on the bed and took a swig from his can. "He punched a kid." Keith was never one to beat around the bush. Carol's face sagged and her shoulders fell in disappointment. "Sounds like the other boy was picking on him, making fun of his shoes. I got a call from the school around 2, had to bring him to the building site, I made him do homework in the office trailer." His latest gig was construction work on a new retail center just north of downtown.

Carol held the bridge of her nose with her eyes closed and let out a sigh. "Please tell me he's not expelled."

"Suspended this time, not next time."

They remained silent for a few moments, Keith staring at Carol and Carol staring through the window into the black night. Either of her parents would have whipped the bejesus out of her in the same situation, and it wasn't as though she had never given the boys a hard smack on the backside when they were especially ill-behaved. But something just didn't feel right about doing that here. It wasn't enough. This was really important.

"Did you punish him?" she asked.

"Not yet, I figured I'd talk with you first."

She paused, contemplating. "What do you think?"

Keith shrugged. "Grounding? Or we could spank him, I'll do it."

She considered for a moment but demurred. "No, I don't want to do that." She stared out the window once more. "Ground the hell out of him, I guess. I'll take care of it," she said before walking back to the kitchen.

Denny was halfway down a page of math problems but stopped and watched her approach. His sandy blond hair hung down over one eye. Carol pulled out a chair, sat down, then gently took the pen out of his hand and set it on the table. She took a deep breath and stared into his eyes for several seconds. "I'm sure it wasn't your fault, Denny-..."

"It wasn't," he jumped in, suddenly engaged in the only part of the discussion where he felt he would had some control. "I wasn't sayin' nothing to him and he starts talkin' about my hightops..."

"Denny." She raised her hand for quiet. "I'm gonna start again because I need for you to hear me loud and clear. I'm sure it wasn't your fault." This time he just kept his eyes on her. "But I'm afraid that doesn't matter. There are times in life where you *know* you're in the right, where you *know* that someone isn't being fair or good to you, but... you just have to take it. You have to take it because something is more important than sticking up for yourself. Because something is more important than teaching them a lesson, or getting them back." His eyes had mostly remained locked on hers but were now inching down toward the table. "This family is more important than your pride, Denny. Your education is more important than your pride." She reached over, put an index finger under his chin and lifted his head to face her again. "You. Have. GOT. To stay in school. You hear me?"

6

His eyes angled downward a bit again as he said, "Yes, ma'am."

"Good." She took a breath and also stared at the table, then looked over at him. "Now... since you *did* hit him..." His eyes turned up to her. "...I sure hope you made it count." She grinned ever so slightly, which made him do the same.

Quietly, he said, "I sure hope so, my hand hurts somethin' awful."

✚

1984 · DOM, AGE SEVEN

Just two months remained in the Branciforte Elementary school year. Miss Theresa sat transfixed, a large sheet of newsprint in her hands, her head shaking slowly side to side. "This kid..." she said to herself. She couldn't stop admiring the care he had taken with every stroke, the perfection of the lighting and shadow, and the baffling lack of corrections. "From God's eyes to his little hands." A soft knock on the door frame behind her, and there stood the prodigy.

"Oh, hi, Dominic," she said while self-consciously setting aside his drawing. "Come on in. I was just looking at your work. It's really good."

"Thank you, Miss Theresa," Dominic said in a monotone that suggested it wasn't the first such compliment he had received.

"Dominic, why does it say, 'Still Taking the Train' at the bottom?"

A slightly surprised look crossed his face. "That's the title," he replied.

Theresa smiled. "Oh, I see." She looked over the piece again and realized that two of the baskets might have looked to him like a locomotive engine. She wanted to probe further into the title's meaning but didn't really have time. "Um, Dominic..." She considered her words for a moment. "Are you happy in my class?"

"Yes." A predictably default answer.

"Okay. Well, the reason I ask is that you... I think maybe you should be in Mrs. Hannigan's class instead of mine." No response. "I mean I

7

love *having you in my class, Dominic, truly, but, well... you're just more advanced than the rest of the students here, you have a gift for art. I don't think you're going to learn very much in my class."*

"Okay." *This was not Dominic's first early graduation, Miss Theresa's class was already two levels above where he would normally be. He didn't know who Mrs. Hannigan was, but he assumed there were bigger kids in her class.*

So it was, all through Dom's early life. As a toddler, he never ate the crayons, he just drew with them. Before his parents had even considered teaching him how to draw shapes and stick figures he was drawing clumsy outlines of abstract shapes inside *things that he saw — the patterns in decorative grasses, refractions that his mother's crystal projected on the wall, the chiaroscuro of an orange. Things that art teachers normally have to fight to make "normal" people see, Dominic was rendering from the start.*

His progressive, life-affirming parents encouraged his abilities as well as they possibly could. All of his schools, even his preschool, were chosen not for their academic credentials but for the strength and vision of their art programs. Predictably, Dom travelled up the ranks at a rapid pace. By the time he started middle school he had been allowed a couple of days a week to sit in with the advanced high school freshman class, and before his tenth grade year he had begun nightly classes at the local university and private critique sessions with a faculty member once a week.

1992 · AGE FIFTEEN

"Impressive as always, kid." Professor Von Geddre was staring at a colorful but unassuming landscape resting on a heavy wooden easel, chewing the gum that Dom had offered when he walked in. The professor's eyes fell in a squint to the lower right corner. "Dom, what's that 'Midnight in the Garden of Evel Knievel' written at the bottom?"

Dom smirked and girded himself for a lecture. "The title, sir."

8

Von Geddre smirked back, adopted a skeptical look. "I assume you realize that objective renderings like this don't usually have titles."

"Yes sir, I know."

"So why bother?"

They had been asking him this question since he first learned to spell. All of Dom's work had titles, no matter how unoriginal, analytical, inconsequential or incomplete. As a child he had started doing it because most of the great works he had been shown had titles and he assumed that it was against the rules not to include one. But by now it had stubbornly developed into a permanent fixture of his work, partly because they had tried to make him stop and he was so hard-headed, but also because...

"I guess I'd have trouble feeling like it was worth the effort if it didn't have a title," he said, looking at the drawing instead of the teacher. "I don't think I could go on creating art if I thought the next piece wouldn't have a unique identity."

"Hm." The professor thought this over. "I suspect that may be a clue to a deeper issue, but I'm not insightful enough at this hour to speculate about such things. Time will tell, I suppose."

They discussed the rest of the piece for a half hour or so, but Von Geddre was starting to feel he was no longer equipped to help Dom progress. He poured a fresh cup of coffee, dropped his gum in the trash and stared out the office window at the red evening sky. "Dom," he said without turning. "Where... well... what do you want to be in ten years?"

Dom's mouth stopped chewing. He realized that although "what do you want to be when you grow up?" was a simple question that every kid had been asked countless times, he himself had never actually been asked. Everyone, including himself, had just taken it for granted that he would be a famous artist. He had never been asked to put it into words, and doing so seemed surprisingly difficult.

"I guess... well... I guess I'll be an artist, right?" he said as if to verify that Von Geddre knew the correct answer and was just withholding it.

The professor shrugged. "I guess. Is that what you want, or what you think other people want?" And just to make sure the third option was available: "Or both?"

Dom looked as deep inside him as he could and saw only the obvious answer. "Both," he said to the wall, then turned to the professor with a bemused and resolved look. "Of course. Both!"

✚

Cape University Professor Evan Johns took a deep breath, removed his glasses and rubbed his reddened eyes. He and Dom were alone in the office adjacent to the painting studio. "I'm afraid I can only sympathize with your lack of experience, Dom. Most artists start with no inspiration other than the works of their creative idols, usually the greatest artists of history." He was very tired, and not very receptive to a whining session. "They start with their merely good ideas and focus mainly on executing them well. The great ideas... they might come later or they might not. It's admirable to shoot for greatness, but dangerous to get frustrated when it doesn't happen."

It was all true, but Johns knew he was wasting his breath. Dom tapped lightly at the arm of his chair with a balled fist. He was staring at the yellowing Rothko poster on the studio wall. "Sure."

The professor hoped that silence might bring the conversation to a close but could sense that the issue would come up again if he didn't try to kill it now, and he knew his explanation didn't really apply in Dom's case anyway. "It goes without saying that your work is excellent. I love the ideas you come up with. The diptych you showed us last month was beautiful. Work like that sells, Dom." An annoyed frown crossed Dom's face and the professor realized the statement was irrelevant. "I guess that's not what you're worried about, is it?"

Dom shook his head slowly. "Nope."

"Selling art is a given — you care only about carving yourself a place in history. How lucky you are to have such a problem." He knew he shouldn't be goading Dom, but it was hard not to poke fun at such an arrogant kid, well-founded as Dom's ego was. Quietly he said, "David wasn't chiselled in a day."

Dom leaned into his hand for a moment, then stood up a little too suddenly and walked quickly toward the door. He stopped there and turned. "Sorry, professor. I, um... I appreciate the advice."

"Take it easy, Dom. I mean it. Relax."

Dom threw a wave over his shoulder and walked out of the studio more in control of himself. Professor Walsh walked in from the outside door at the other end. "What's new, Evan?"

"The usual." Johns stroked his forehead. "Golden boy wants to know why he isn't Rembrandt yet."

Walsh pulled a mug out of a cabinet and poured a cup of coffee. "You did say he was the most gifted student you ever saw."

"Oh, he is, Gary, by far. But he knows that's the case without anyone telling him, and he's about to explode because he isn't living up to the expectations he and everyone else have set for him. It's starting to get me worried. I don't really care whether he finishes his projects, but he's been closing himself off more and more."

"Mm. Well hell, maybe that anger will inspire him."

"Yeah, maybe. But it's inspiring the wrong behavior right now." The professor was twiddling a cigarette in his hand that he wasn't allowed to smoke in the studio. "He's always been capable of shooting holes in other people's work, pointing out things they might have corrected or thought of, but... lately he's become belligerent about it, insulting. He's taking his own frustrations out on everyone in the class..."

"Bullshit." Dom said quietly from the side of the room, where he was sitting on a stool well outside the circle. He was staring sideways at the painting on the wall with a disgusted look on his face, shaking his head slowly. Less quietly: "That's bullshit, Dave — it's a cop-out. There's nothing wrong with using the same idea twice, but pretending that it's two ideas... it's bullshit."

The professor sighed. This scenario was starting to become routine, and it was getting tiresome.

Dave West, normally difficult to perturb, was perturbed. "It's not the same idea, you dick..."

"Who the hell cares?" Eddie Carrick piped up from the opposite side of the group. "This is just Sir Dominic's usual artsier-than-thou soap box."

"Eddie..." Professor Johns tried to interject.

"I mean heaven forbid any of us have our own opinions about our own work," Eddie continued. "Hey, I think ol' Dom should just re-write our textbooks so we'll know what to think about everything!"

"Oh, shut the *fuck* up, Carrick," Dom snapped. "Nobody gives a flying rat's ass about your-"

"Oh, I think you should come *shut* me the fuck up, Winters..."

The professor jumped in. "Hey, that's enough!"

"No, seriously," Eddie said as he hopped up from his stool and walked in front of the class. "I'd like to take a little poll — who here wants to hear more of Dom's feedback on our work?"

The professor was getting a headache. "Eddie..."

"Well? Anyone?" Most people were looking at the floor or the wall, and no one was raising their hand. "I'm not seeing any hands here."

Dom was looking out the window, pretending not to care, but he knew what the vote count was. He looked over at Alex, who frowned and shrugged back at him; what difference would it make for his best friend to raise his hand? Better to ignore the whole thing.

Dom wasn't thrilled with himself as it was. He wasn't thrilled with his life. He wasn't thrilled with his or anyone else's work, but to say that he wasn't thrilled with Eddie Carrick would be to say that the ocean isn't dry. Even back when Dom's criticism was helpful and interesting, jealous Eddie would invariably mock, challenge or otherwise irritate Dom, and for the most part the class disliked Eddie for it. This made it all the more painful when they failed to take Dom's side in the "vote."

The professor was at his wit's end. "All right LOOK," he said as he stood up and walked to the front, looking harshly at Eddie and pointing like a spear at the stool Eddie had come from. Eddie sat. "I've had it with this childish crap. Not ten minutes into critique and already you're yelling across the room. No more petty bickering in my studio, *period.*" He looked over at Dom, still staring out the window, then back at Eddie, who was glaring sideways at Dom. He took a deep breath and said, "You know what, forget it. This isn't going to work right now. Go home we'll pick this up on Wednesday."

Everyone in the middle looked at each other in confusion but didn't move. Dom looked slowly over at the frustrated class, then stood up and walked toward the door. "No, don't worry about it — I'm going."

"What a martyr," Eddie mumbled as Dom walked past.

Dom froze just for a moment in the doorway, clenched both fists together, then released them and walked out.

Alex jabbed him in the arm. "Hey, jack-ass, did you hear what I said? You owe me a back-flop."

Dom was absentmindedly returning art supplies to his storage bin. "Hm? Oh, damn." For Alex's sake he feigned disappointment, but clearly wasn't interested. "Yeah, okay, I'll do it this weekend."

"Nah, dude, *today.* Karen and I are hitting the Hole after lab and you're coming with."

"Lex, I'm really not in the mood right-"

"That's why I insist." Alex pulled Dom's shoulder to the side to face him head-on. "You need something to take your mind off of this shit,

Dom. And if I have to..." He grabbed and twisted Dom's arm up into his back.

Dom grunted. "Okay, fucktard. Enough."

Alex released, pushed him away and backed toward the studio door with a smirk on his face. "4 PM sharp or I tell Karen about the bed-wetting."

Bell's Quarry has been abandoned longer than Cape Johns has existed, a two hundred year old eyesore-turned-landmark. Not quite interesting or accessible enough to draw tourists, it had been left to grow wild (and remarkably beautiful when compared to most of the Cape), marked only by the battered, gray historical site placard at the base of the trail leading to the quarry's best photo-op. It was a path less traveled that led Dom & Company almost weekly to one of the more hidden-away areas, a stair-stepped cliff blocked at all angles by weeds and wildflowers, overlooking a circular pool of seemingly untouched blue-green water. They called it The Hole.

Alex had actually discovered this oasis with a couple of classmates while he was still an undergrad, and it had quickly become the secret clubhouse of the art department's upper echelon, of which Dom was the de facto leader. Alex lost a rather foolish bet to Dom not long after they had joined themselves at the hip, and a back-flop into the pond was the painful result. This masochistic act had been the penalty for many subsequent bets and was always attended by at least a few friendly art school hecklers. A couple of times they had even brought large white score cards that they lifted up in unison, which made the event all the more monumental for Alex and Dom, who, through their competitive nature, had changed it from a foolish punishment into a test of mettle, the measure of which was how spectacularly one could abuse one's body. The first flop was from a mere eight feet up, but each jump had quickly given way to the next highest platform until both contestants became limited by the tallest perch available, nearly thirty feet over the water.

"Boy, does that water look c-c-c-cold," Alex said with his arms folded across his chest in a fake shiver, throwing a sideways glance at Dom. "I sure am glad I don't have to test it ass-first."

Karen laughed. "This my favorite part, the anticipation. Prolonging the inevitable SMACK," she said as she slapped Dom with both hands hard on the back, "into the icy depths of Arctic Cape Johns."

Dom was unfazed. "Hell, I'd be back-flopping this shit whether I owed you a flop or not. That water's gonna be soft as a bunny rabbit."

"As if," Alex said. "Get to it, Mister Tough as Nails."

Dom kicked off his flops and doffed his t-shirt, the absence of which emphasized the dried paint and plaster on his forearms. He climbed the precarious hand-holds that led to the precipice. The sun was blazing. He could feel sweat beading on his skin. The water really was going to feel good, and in fact Dom felt great for the first time in weeks, far away from his art life, surrounded by his best friends at the least industrial spot in all of Cape Johns. He breathed deeply, taking it all in.

"Jump, dickhead!" Alex yelled.

Dom grinned, then looked down at the water and dug his toes into the rocky edge. In a maneuver he had practiced almost a dozen times now, he squatted as low as he could, reached his hands high behind him (flicking a middle finger in Alex's direction), leaned forward and jumped as high as he could into the air, arms stretching forward as though he was a super-hero. Dom always wished he could stretch this moment into slow-motion, the incomprehensibly short spot at the dive's apex where he really was flying through the air, high above his ultimate destination. The entire process was an exhilarating joy — straightening out like a board, leaning slowly into the dive, letting the arms float outward of their own accord to form a cross with the slowly rotating body as the head comes up from the bottom to face the sun. The last leg of the journey downward, a combination of the serene beauty of the clear afternoon sky and the furious buffeting of wind through the hair and past the ears, would have been equally enjoyable were it not for the terrible apprehension of contact with the water.

This apprehension seemed to grow with each such jump because contact with the water was so excruciatingly shocking and painful that it made one completely forget the joy that preceded it. Only the soft comfort of the cool water underneath could soothe the bruised skin and immediate headache caused by the impact. Dom and Alex agreed that passing out at this point would be ideal, but the chaotic rush of water never allowed for that possibility. Although an outside viewer would never know it, screaming into the water after the impact was as inevitable as blinking during a sneeze.

Dom had outdone himself. His landing was picture-perfect, and the pop of his back striking the water was so loud that Karen jumped in spite of herself. It was so spectacular, in fact, that everyone momentarily forgot that it was funny, involuntarily worried about Dom's welfare. Adding to this concern was the delay before he emerged — Dom seemed to stay below the surface longer each time he made these jumps, usually because he had grown more and more accustomed to the shock and was determined not to let it get the best of him, but this time because he was further enjoying the distraction that the sensations of nature provided.

He finally surfaced, looked up at the cheering crowd and yelled at the top of his lungs, "WINTERS ELEVEN, QUARRY ZERO!"

The group was still laughing when Dom reached the platform again. A carelessly-rolled joint was handed to him. Though the collision was more painful than it had ever been, Dom felt great. The back-flop had further wrested him from the torment that had been mounting in his soul for weeks.

"Nice, very nice," said Mike Edmond, a former roommate of Dom's. Karen exhaled smoke and said, "Nice hell, that was the best one yet," she said with raised eyebrows.

"Not the funniest, though," Deirdre said from the top of the cliff. She had been on her high school's diving team and was the only one among them who could actually make a work of art out of these jumps. "Alex's mangled sideways flop was a fucking riot. I still can't believe you're not deaf in that ear."

"Deaf-schmeaf, hearing is overrated," Alex scoffed. "You just wait until I lose another bet and I do the next jump left-handed."

"Hardy har har," Dom said as he grabbed Alex from behind in a bear-lock. Alex was struggling to free himself when a new voice emanated from the trail. It was the voice of Eddie Carrick.

"Nice move, genius," he said. "Who the hell taught you to dive, a crash test dummy?" He was joined by a couple of thoroughly pierced girls who Dom didn't recognize, the three of them clearly dressed to make themselves at home in the water.

All of Dom's troubles suddenly returned with a vengeance. It was infuriating enough that Eddie was here at all — he had been carefully left in the dark about the Hole — and the fact that he was so boldly prodding Dom about what he mistakenly thought was a botched dive was icing on the cake.

No one in Dom's camp was sure what to say, so shocked they were to see Eddie there on the cliff. Finally Karen spoke up. "He did that on purpose, you moron."

Eddie laughed as he replied, "Oh, I'm so sure. I know lots of people who like to enter the water sideways." He dropped his towel and pulled one of his shoes off. Everyone else was still staring in disbelief. They had been using this spot exclusively for so long that they sincerely felt that it belonged to them. Eddie looked around at the stunned faces. "Yeah, good to be here, thanks for the invitation."

Dom's rage was growing with each passing moment. He hated every inch of Eddie Carrick, and he could barely contain his fury enough to calmly say, "You... are not welcome... here."

Eddie had been leaning over to reach his other shoe, but now he paused, straightened up slowly and said through narrowed eyes, "I... don't give a shit... asswipe."

Dom's body was tensed all over. His arms were hanging at his sides and he was clenching and unclenching his fists. Eddie's companions stopped making themselves comfortable and stared alternately at Dom and Eddie.

Alex also disliked Eddie, but not as much as Dom did, and besides that he was as non-confrontational as they come. Sensing that Dom was about to lose his cool, he attempted to intervene. "Eddie, just go find some other spot, okay?"

"FUCK you, Alex, it's a free country," Eddie replied without taking his eyes off Dom. He was cocky enough in class that he knew he couldn't give in to Dom's demands, but he also knew that Dom meant business and Eddie honestly did not want to fight — Dom had a distinct height advantage, lanky as he was. Dom sensed this and was all the more eager to free his anger on Eddie's person. The punctured girls seemed uneasy about the whole situation and clearly wanted to move on.

"Hey, let's just go somewhere else," one of them said quietly to Eddie.

"This is *not* Mount Saint Dominic, goddamn it!" Eddie yelled as he batted her outstretched hand away. "These assholes do not own the fucking quarry!"

Dom took a slow step forward, ready to leap like a cat at Eddie. "You've got one more chance, Carrick. Get out of my sight."

Eddie paused, tensing himself, unable to think through the adrenaline that was coursing through him. Through clenched teeth he said, "Go... fuck... yourself."

Dom had never thrown a real punch in his life, and from the lack of a reaction and the unmistakable crunch of bone in his nose it sounded like Eddie had never received one. It hurt both of them like hell, but the pain only fueled Dom's rage. His next punch went through Eddie's flailing arms and landed in the side of his throat. Coughing and moaning, he dove diagonally past Dom, toward the edge of the cliff. Dom was too blinded with anger to consider the danger and was moving too determinedly for Alex or Mike's desperate attempts to stop him. He landed one more punch into Eddie's stomach before Eddie rolled sideways off the cliff. Karen and one of the unknown girls shrieked. Dom's momentum landed him on the ground with his head looking over the edge. Alex and Mike fell in beside him and the three of them watched as Eddie, curled into a fetal position with blood streaming down his face and neck, toppled end over end and landed like a rag doll in the water.

Deirdre cried, "Oh my god," just before leaping from the cliff and diving like a spear into the water to Eddie's right. Alex quickly followed, feet first, aiming behind and to the left of Eddie. They could only just be seen converging on him through the rippling water before the three of them emerged, Alex and Deirdre kicking and paddling furiously for the bank.

"Is he breathing?!" Mike yelled down at them. Their lack of an answer and rushed movements indicated that he wasn't, and Mike darted down the side path that led to the bottom while pulling a cell phone out of his pocket, mumbling, "shit, shit, shit..."

Karen was also watching the whole scene from the edge, paralyzed. She was a strong person, brimming with kindness and character, but not the most reliable in crisis situations. She was trying to snap out of her shock as she looked over and realized that Dom had not moved since Eddie went over. "Dom?"

His mind was having a hard time registering what had just happened, and what was happening now. He couldn't seem to bring himself to focus, the past sixty seconds were a total blank.

Karen tried again. "Dom, are you okay? Dom?" She looked down at the commotion below. Alex and Deirdre had pulled Eddie onto the bank and were trying to gently revive him, his eyes had opened and he seemed to be gathering his wits. Mike was talking on his phone beside them, pacing back and forth.

"Yes... yeah... NO, no, no, it's not like attempted murder or anything — they just got in a fist fight, it was an accident." Mike was doing his best to paint a rosy picture on the situation now that Eddie was evidently going to be okay. "No, he didn't really... he didn't really push him off the cliff, not on purpose. He was just angry and they were fighting and the other guy *fell* off the cliff."

"Eddie? Can you hear me?" Dierdre was patting him gently on the cheek.

Eddie was staring skyward with his blood-tinged mouth hanging open. His nose was still bleeding, but not profusely. "Yeah," he said quietly. "Yeah."

"How do you feel, Eddie?" Alex said and held up three fingers. "How many fingers am I holding up?"

Eddie looked down at the hand and back at Alex. "Twenty-two," he answered. Alex and Deirdre looked at each other skeptically and Eddie grinned. "Ask a stupid question..." He seemed to be turning back into Eddie again.

Alex pursed his lips and sat back on a rock. "I think he'll be all right."

Up at the top, Karen was still trying to bring Dom back to earth. His face was hanging over the edge but didn't appear to be focused on the scene below. "Dom, I think he's okay. Dom."

He was locked in place. Nothing was going in or out. Nothing was happening inside. He couldn't seem to gather enough willpower to make himself move or speak. Karen reached out and stroked his arm and continued to speak to him to no avail. After a couple of minutes she yelled down to the bottom, "Alex, I think something's wrong with Dom!"

Eddie, who was now sitting up, was affronted. "Something's wrong with Dom? The guy who just kicked Eddie off a cliff?"

"Shut up Eddie," Alex said, then yelled to Karen, "What do you mean?"

"Well," she was unsure of her words. "He, ah... he's just not... doing anything. He seems frozen."

"Okay, we'll come up." He turned back to Eddie. "All right, casualty, let's see if you can stand." He and Dierdre helped Eddie to his feet. Eddie was a little unstable, but strong enough to walk with their support. He seemed to lean a bit unnecessarily on Dierdre's shoulder. She either didn't notice or wasn't bothered enough to object.

Alex and Karen had finally managed to coerce Dom into an upright position by the time police and paramedics arrived, but he was still staring into nothingness and hadn't spoken a word. The other two girls were gone — either they cared enough to go get help or they didn't want to be around when the authorities came to find out what had happened. The medics insisted on checking Dom over before any attempt at questioning was made. Eddie insisted on not being checked over or questioned at all.

He seemed to be arguing with the officer in charge. "I know what happened, asshole." He was fairly calm, but clearly getting pissed off. "I was there, remember?"

"Hey, don't get *smart* with me, you little shit," the officer snapped. "I'm trying to tell you what your options are here. This guy could have killed you and you're just going to let him slide?"

"That's what I said, now piss off." Eddie walked over to his bag and started gathering his things together. The officer shook his head and indicated to the other two cops that they could leave. Since no charges were going to filed he seemed content to give up on any further investigation. If the victim wouldn't lay any blame, it wasn't his problem.

Alex watched all of this while Karen stroked Dom's non-fighting hand. Eddie looked over at Dom with a face of stone, then glanced the same way at Alex for a moment before walking away.

The medic couldn't find anything physically wrong with Dom other than a heavily bruised hand and couple of light scuffs. "I think he'll be okay," he said to Karen. "But we should take him to the hospital anyway and keep an eye on him until he snaps out of this."

"No," Dom said, still otherwise catatonic.

Everyone looked at him in surprise. "What?" Karen said. "Dom, are you okay?" No answer. "Dom, we need to make sure you're okay."

"No," Dom said again as he pulled his feet beneath him and stood up. He paused for a moment as if to make sure standing was feasible, then started walking down the exit trail, ignoring his bag and clothes.

"Dom!" Karen yelled after him and they all followed. Dom walked straight down the trail and around Alex's car, opened the door and sat down in the passenger seat, still staring straight ahead with his mouth slightly open.

Everyone looked at each other, not sure what to do. The medic caught up and said to Karen, "Look, he's probably going to be okay — he's just suffering from a little bit of shock right now. I think he should probably come with us, but if he's alert enough to deny our help, there's nothing we can do." He pulled out his wallet and held a card out for Karen. "I suggest you call the hospital after you get him home, make a doctor appointment, maybe speak with a hospital counsellor."

Karen took the card, looking as confused as the rest of the group. "Okay, thanks." The other medic had packed up already and the two of them drove away in their ambulance.

Alex spoke up. "Okay. Well. Um, I'll drive him home and stay with him for awhile, see if he snaps out of it. Dierdre, can you drop Mike off?"

Dierdre, who had never witnessed the Dom/Eddie rivalry firsthand, seemed less confused than annoyed. "Alex, what the hell was that all about? Was it really that big a deal that Eddie found out about the Hole?"

Alex was a little surprised by the question. He opened his mouth, paused, and looked over at Dom. "Look... Dierdre, you have to understand that Eddie is constantly badgering Dom just because he's jealous —"

"And that justifies pushing him off a *cliff*?" she spat back, hands on hips. Now that the situation had levelled off and she had time to consider Dom's actions, she was starting to get pissed. "No, Alex, it doesn't fucking work that way. You don't..." She leaned over to yell through the car window at Dom. "YOU don't get to kill someone just because he's an asshole, Dom, I don't care how much you fucking hate him." She stood back up and looked around at the rest. "Is no one gonna back me up on this?"

The others seemed conflicted. They were all in Dom's painting class and knew all too well where Dom's rage came from, but Dierdre had a point. They stared at each other and then over at Dom, who now seemed even more vacantly distressed than he was before.

"Selfish bullshit," Dierdre said to herself as she turned and walked to her car without inviting Mike to get in with her. She drove away quickly.

They stood in silence for a few moments, then Karen spoke up, "Okay, I'll drop Mike off and then join you at Dom's."

"Right," Alex said, and they all departed, still dazed.

You don't get to kill someone just because he's an asshole, Dom. He couldn't push those words out of his mind. Over and over the awful scene played out in his head. Most of it was a blur; he had been so charged with adrenaline that the details were hard to pick out. The only aspect that was crystal clear was the final rage-induced charge that nearly made a violent murderer of Dominic Winters. *What are you doing?* His right foot had slipped in the sand, but the loss of balance was overcome by the adrenaline that was coursing through him. *How could you do something like that?* The pulsing of blood through his system had created a rushing sound in his ears. *Weren't you going to be world-famous?* The last step was boosted by a root that happened to swell just below his left foot, launching him forward. *Were you really on the edge of greatness, or were you just going to burn with frustration until you destroyed something?* Eddie was so covered with sweat that Dom got virtually no grip when he grabbed at the torso. The only thing unclear in his memory was the intent — Dom just wasn't sure what he had meant to do. *You don't get to kill someone just because you can't quench your desire to be an artistic legend.*

"Dom, I'm going to pull in here and get some gas, okay?" Dom's stare remained unchanged, and Alex guessed that the stare would remain in place until he got back. He put $7 into the tank (all he had on him) and went inside to pay. Although the line inside was unusually long for a Friday afternoon, Alex was inside for less than five minutes, so it was that much more surprising that Dom's seat was empty when Alex got back to the car.

"DOM!" He looked around in every direction he could guess that Dom might have wandered off, but saw nothing.

Dom's mental shock had faded enough to allow for a combination of rational thought and vicious depression. Still donning only trunks, sandals and a paint-spattered t-shirt, he had wandered onto one of the more run-down strips in town and into perhaps the most run-down bar available.

You're no better an artist than the asshole you nearly killed. You think you're a sleeping legend just because you have a knack for, what, arranging things? Rendering? Real artists ship. Real artists triumph. You've painted, sculpted and drawn your fingers to the bone for twenty years. If inspiration was going to strike, it would have struck by now. You're not great and you never will be. You're just a selfish, arrogant hack.

In front of Dom sat his sixth shot of the cheapest whiskey in the house. His eyes had seldom moved from the "L.H. ♥'s A.J." inscription on the wooden bar top in front of him. A cheesy country ballad played on the jukebox. Pool table cracks and the voices of random yokels checkered the air. A broken bottle and some shouting preceded a near-scuffle toward the back. Dom was oblivious to it all — haunting images and belligerent voices dominating his concentration — until an unnecessarily loud comment nearby yanked him back to reality.

"...Yeah boy, I wish I was better'n everybody else," said a charismatic voice four empty seats to Dom's left. The voice was facing the bartender, who didn't seem inclined to encourage the conversation. A second voice one more seat over was happy to.

"I tell you what," said the higher-pitched Southern voice, "we simple folk sure are lucky them genius kids is around." The grizzled 50-year-old was rolling a cigarette to replace the fading butt hanging from his lower lip. "I just don't know what I'd do if they wasn't here to tell us low-class shitheads what buildings not to tear down and where we can smoke our cancer sticks."

The hair on the back of his neck rose along with his pulse. Dom was staring alternately at the inscription and the floor when he realized that his Birkenstocks had probably given him away. No townie would be caught dead in a brand-name sandal. He didn't dare look over to see what he was up against or give them a cue to badger him further. That would be pointless anyway; any bar patron who had the balls to pick fights with strangers would know better than to pick one that they might lose. Dom was tall, but hardly intimidating.

The bartender, a burly but sedate man with dark hair and a gray horseshoe moustache, had walked over casually to stand in front of Dom, staring at the basketball game playing on a blurry TV in the corner while wiping out a couple of mugs. Quietly he said, "Son, I think it would be best if you'd move on."

Dom looked slowly up at him, but the bartender kept his eyes on the tube. Dom pulled out his wallet, looked through his bills and realized he was short. "Um..."

The bartender reached over and took the wad out of Dom's hand and tossed it in the tip jar, then turned back to the game. "Go on."

Dom stood up and walked toward the door as humbly as he could. On any other night he might have had a hard time walking in a straight line, but the adrenaline now coursing through his veins steadied his steps.

"Whattsa matter, boy?" the first voice called after him. "You too good for us grunts? How about if I shine them fancy sandals? I might even throw in a blow-job!" The last thing Dom heard was the second voice cackling with laughter.

It was a bit chilly outside for beach attire, the air and streets now coated with evening mist. Dom's shock had mostly been replaced with alcohol by now, but his depression had done nothing but increase since Eddie's feet left the cliff's edge. He walked in a forlorn stupor in the direction of his apartment, having spent his cab fare on whiskey (not that cabs would bother with a neighborhood like this at such a late hour). Only the sound of Dom's clumsy steps filled the air.

He probably wouldn't have been any less helpless had he been alert and sober. A 2x4 to the back of the head may as well have been a lead pipe for the effect that it had on Dom's skull. He was only dimly aware of falling to the wet ground, but his convulsing body ensured that he was aware of the beating he was being given.

It didn't last long, just enough for him to learn whatever lesson he was supposed to be receiving. Intense pain coursed through his trunk. Dom's consciousness fell at pace with his breathing. In the moments afterward he could have sworn he distantly heard Eddie's voice.

✛

On another night, Richard "Dixie" Park might have walked out of the bar behind that art school shit-bag and kicked the piss out of him. But fuck it, he wasn't in the mood. He licked and sealed his roughly rolled cig, set it on the cardboard coaster beside his half-empty Bud, and folded down the top of the tobacco pouch before pocketing it and pulling out a lighter. Earl the bartender had already started walking slowly toward him. He spoke in a calm but firm baritone.

"Can't smoke that in here, Dixie. State law."

Dixie closed his eyes and sighed, dropping the cigarette and lighter on the bar. "God dammit," he said pointedly. Without moving his head, he opened his eyes and stared at the bartender, tossing options around in his mind: light it up anyway, fuck state law; raise hell, probably sleep in jail (second time this month); or drink his beer and smoke outside — just what the "civilized" world expected of him. Earl didn't take no shit, so Dixie would be unceremoniously escorted to the door with either of those first two options. Checkmate. He dropped his gaze and picked up the beer.

The dude beside him spoke up again. "You drive for Heartland, right?"

Dixie, who had momentarily forgotten about the previous conversation, glanced vaguely in his direction. "Yeah. I mean no... mechanic. For Heartland."

"Right, right." A pause. "You guys are mostly Freightliner, yeah?"

Small talk, good grief. Dixie paused a sec before mumbling a response. "Mostly International, a few Freightliners." He picked up his cig and lighter, stood up, and guzzled the rest of his beer. "What I owe ya, Earl?"

Earl looked down at a tab behind the bar. "Six Buds, twelve bucks."

Dixie dropped a five and counted out lots of ones. "Thanks Earl, take 'er easy." He then turned to his burly bar friend, and started to say something but paused again, this time searching. "Uh, Dave?"

"Dan."

"Dan, right." He pointed his thumb at himself, "Dixie. Later on, Dan." He turned and walked gingerly out of the bar and turned down the street, antsy and surly.

It was chillier than he expected outside, and the denim jacket over his barely buttoned Hawaiian shirt wasn't quite cutting it, so he walked quickly. Where the royal fuck had he left his sister's car? He paused to yank the cig and lighter out, took a long drag and put the lighter away, squinting down the street, looking for that stupid antenna tennis ball. Nothing. Shit, that's right, it was around the next corner.

He pulled the keys out before rounding the corner into a dark alley where the car was, then immediately tripped over the outstretched legs of a homeless man in a sleeping bag, falling onto damp concrete beside the sludgy footprint of a dumpster, his cigarette skittering forward into the crevice under an abandoned tire. The occupant of the sleeping bag grunted and mumbled something unintelligible.

"WHAT IN THE MOTHER FUCK," Dixie yelled as he sprang up and looked behind him. The blue sleeping bag was shifting in the dim light from a nearby street lamp. "YOU FUCKIN' PIECE A GARBAGE!" he screamed just before throwing everything he had into a soccer kick to the knees. The trapped man let out an equally loud wail of shock and agony, not comprehending what was happening. More simultaneous fury and anguish ensued as Dixie unleaded a continued barrage of kicks while his victim writhed and rolled before attempting to climb out of the bag and up the nearby wall. At that point, Dixie squared up and planted a running kick directly into the man's exposed stomach, sending his target out onto the sidewalk. By this point there was no more significant noise coming from the wretch — instead, he was gasping as fast and hard as he could for air, with an occasional whimper or cough. Blood fell from his mouth onto the ground.

The faintest pang of regret lit deep inside of Dixie but was quickly snuffed out by anger and determination. Panting, heart pounding, almost dizzy from the intensity of his actions, he lowered his head and stepped forward, not entirely sure what he would do next but fairly sure he wasn't done. Realizing, however, that he and the homeless man were now exposed to stronger ambient light on a sidewalk not far from residential buildings, immediately after making a shitload of noise, Dixie caught himself short. He glanced around, down the street both ways and up into the building windows, seeing no activity but sensing unwanted attention on him nonetheless. Slowly, he stepped backward into the shadow of the building and turned back toward the alley. He picked up the car keys and his still-lit cigarette. It was wet on one side, but still smokeable.

The kicking incident had half wrested Dixie from his drunkenness, and he made it back to the apartment complex with only a couple of parking taps on either end of the journey. He ambled up the cracked cement walkway and up the stairs to his sister's place. Pulling out his keys as he approached, he looked down to find the right one but failed to stop walking and bumped his head into the door. "GOD, fuck," he yelled before taking a deep breath, finding the key and pushing the door open. It swung all the way inward and banged into the adjacent wall, keys rattling in the deadbolt.

"God dammit, Dixie, knock it off!" he heard from the other room. Dixie let out a "Pssh" sound and crabbily waved the complaint away. The apartment was relatively dark, lit only by random electronic displays and a smattering of moonlight. He stumbled into the kitchen and opened up one cabinet and then another before grabbing a half-drunk bottle of Tvarscki vodka and loudly dropping it onto the counter. He then went back to the cupboard for a glass, pushing various dishes loudly around, when the voice popped up again.

"Son... of... a... BITCH," his sister yelled just before rounding the corner into the kitchen, flipping on the light, wearing a tattered, oversized Titans football jersey. Pattie was a slightly overweight brunette in her mid 30's, and she looked even more frazzled than usual. She marched straight at Dixie, stopping two feet in front of him. "What the FUCK are you doing? I gotta wake up for work in three hours, you piece a shit!"

That got Dixie's attention — he stopped his search for a glass and stared pointedly at her before slamming the cabinet door. "What the fuck did you just call me?" he asked, closing the gap slowly until his face was inches from hers. "Bitch, we're *family*. If I'm a piece a shit" — he shoved her — "YOU'RE a piece a shit!" Pattie fell gracelessly backwards through the doorway of the kitchen onto the wood laminate floor of the dining area, her head knocking a chair into the table. She kept her eyes on him, chin out in defiance, but she was obviously shaken.

Pattie lifted herself calmly to a standing position. Her eyes were reddening, but she kept them locked on her brother. "No, Dixie," she said quietly. "Just you." Then she walked away to her bedroom and shut the door.

Dixie leaned against the counter, momentarily staring, stone faced, at the vacancy left by his sister. He turned to glance at the cabinet, then the vodka bottle. He grabbed the latter, turned off the light, and walked out of the kitchen to the living area, pulling tobacco, lighter and wallet out to drop them onto the coffee table, then falling into the tattered, vinyl-covered couch — his sleeping quarters — and unscrewing the cap of the bottle. He took a strong swig, winced, and wiped off his mouth.

Dixie stared into space for a bit. Then he looked over at the wallet, splayed open on the coffee table. Stared at it for a long time. Considered pulling the tattered old photo out again, but... he figured he didn't need to. His memory was good enough.

Light. A bright, white light changed to flashing blue. "Hey. Buddy." The sound of a car engine nearby. "HEY." Footsteps, then a firm poke in Dom's ribs. "You conscious?" His aching eyes opened slightly. He tasted blood in his mouth. "You need to get up, kid."

Dom still wasn't sure what was going on. He painfully lifted his head and craned his neck to look up at a stocky cop holding a night stick. "Up," the man repeated. It took all of Dom's strength and endurance to force himself into a kneeling position. He coughed some of the blood out of his mouth and onto the sidewalk underneath him. His face and shirt were wet. His head and a lot of his body hurt like hell, and he could feel a chip in one of his front teeth.

"What's... going on?" he asked. He was trying to kick his brain into gear, but the searing pain and blinding lights weren't helping.

"You are, get moving," the officer spat back, then gave Dom another prod in the back. "There's a shelter two blocks that way." He pointed down the street in the direction opposite Dom's original course.

Dom was starting to remember who he was, though he was still unclear why a policeman was telling him to go to a homeless shelter. "I don't... I don't need a shelter, my apartment is-"

"You got any ID?" the man interrupted. Dom was surprised to discover that he did in fact have a wallet (more evidence that he hadn't been randomly mugged). He started to pull out his driver's license before it dawned on him that his school ID would better represent him at that moment. He handed it to the cop, whose first response was, "Where did you get this?"

Dom didn't understand the question. "What do you mean? At school."

The officer shined his light into Dom's face, then back at the ID. "What the hell are you doing out here, this late at night? What happened to your face?"

Dom didn't have a short answer for this and didn't care to recite the whole story, which would undoubtedly cause a barrage of time-wasting paperwork. "I just... I don't know, I just ended up down here."

A pause. "And?"

"Oh." The bruises and blood. "I got into a... little scuffle with a friend of mine."

"A friend did this?" The cop was annoyed with the situation — it would have made things so much easier if Dom was just a transient.

"Yeah. Look, it's... over and done with, no big deal. Can I just be on my way?" Dom was now lucid enough to have some idea of his rights.

The cop paused again and looked up and down the street. "I don't want to see you down here again, Misterrr..." He looked down at the card. "Winters. This is a rough spot. People in this area don't care for university students." Those people apparently included this policeman.

It was almost over, so Dom regained an obedient tone. "I know. I won't be back."

The cop handed the ID back and said, "Go straight home and clean yourself up."

✚

A Lens on Humanity, from the Eyes of a Child

Modern history is peppered with so-called "child prodigies" of abstract art. The legitimacy of that label is subjective at best and specious at worst; more hype than talent. Parents, friends and buyers alike may be prone to the aggrandizement of babes who show an above-average aptitude for visual sensibilities or creativity. In nearly all cases, the stated talent is more felt *than seen — an interpretation of the child's supposed vision rather than a plain demonstration of their skill.*

But... not always. Once in a "Starry Night" moon, a child comes along who demonstrates a shocking and unequivocal level of artistic capability. Dominic Winters of Brighton, Connecticut was reportedly drawing well before he could walk. Only the boy wasn't drawing the people and objects in front of him, he was rendering the broader shapes that their surfaces created: light and shadow, groups of like colors, even textures. It was as though someone failed to explain to him how children are supposed to draw, so young Dom instead rendered that which art educators every-where struggle to teach their students to see.

"It took us awhile to realize what was happening," his mother Jacqueline told us. "At first we were worried that something was wrong with his vision, even though we couldn't see any other symptoms of that." Instead, they decided that he merely had an unusual preference for how to apply lines to paper. It wasn't until Dom's father Tony discovered the similarity between a golden blob on the paper and a similar shape of sunlight cast across the back of their cat that they realized that Dom's marks were more than just abstract nothings.

Even still, it wasn't until Dom had fully outpaced the artistic abilities of his parents — at around age four — that they began to realize the depth of his talent. By this point, Dom was crafting complex scenes with multiple subjects and reasonably accurate lighting, and some of these were fictitious in nature, with subjects accurately rendered from Dom's memory. Mr. and Mrs. Winters had little experience with the art world, but they knew that they needed help . . .

. . . Young Dominic, now twelve, had already accumulated a wide range of acclaim when he secured and began developing his first professional art showing. Dominic's surrealist oil painting series "Filter" shows us the world as it appears through the eyes of different types of people, each piece illustrating a scene simultaneously as it would appear through an objective view and through the mind of its subject (as depicted from behind, with an empty gap where most of the subject's head would be): a well-dressed man sees price tags and ratings attached to everything and everyone; an African American boy sees padlocks and bars guarding even the food on the table before him; a blond woman sees only predators and sleaze among the males in her purview. Not the sort of psychological insight one expects from a preteen, but Dominic has a great deal of intimate human study under his belt, having spent dozens of hours observing . . .

. . . Dominic spoke with fellow artist and NYC curator Bernhard Hastings in an on-camera interview as he was wrapping up the show last June. "I can't literally see how other people view the world, of course, and I don't pretend to really know how they see things around them. But I spent time with a couple dozen people fitting these roles and I was able to get a sense of how the world might seem different to them."

"Filter" consists of nineteen oil on canvas pieces hanging at the Orlam Gallery, 305 7th Ave. The opening will take place on Friday, September 10th, at 8 PM, and the exhibit will run through the end of the month. Some works are still available for purchase as of this writing.

✚

Dom turned away from the irritated police officer and winced as he took his first steps. He suspected that at least one rib was cracked. Pain and coldness kept his arms crossed over his abdomen. Hunched over and limping, he made his way toward home. Either from necessity or boredom, the belligerent voices returned...

Does it matter who did it? You deserved a beating, not for what you did to Eddie but for why. You didn't attack him, you attacked yourself, you attacked your own ineptitude. Maybe it isn't even your fault — maybe your parents coddled your talent too much, maybe there were just too many cooks.

It's too late to matter now.

His wallet had made it into Alex's car, but Dom's keys had been dropped into his backpack when they left for the Hole, and that backpack was in Karen's car. Dom did not live in a nice building, and to ask one of his neighbors to let him in at 3 AM would mean risking more abuse. He decided to climb the fire escape and wait for morning, which was an unusually difficult task in such a damaged state.

After several struggling minutes he finally hefted himself up onto the platform and waited for his breath and renewed pain to die down. Thanks to the climb he was warm again for the moment, but it occurred to him that sleeping outside in shorts and a t-shirt might leave him in much worse condition than he was already in. He wasn't sure he cared.

Does it matter if you live through this? Is there anything left to live for? You don't know how to live a normal life, a life that isn't dominated by art, a life that doesn't lead to fame, to an entire chapter in the annals of art history. You've never been normal and you never will be.

He lifted his eyes for a moment and looked around him in an attempt to escape the voice. The dim blues and grays left by the moonlight created a futuristic, geometric vortex inside the corridor. Instinctively he considered the scene from an artistic viewpoint. He couldn't help it.

You can't do it. You won't ever be able to turn that off. You'll never be able to forget that you failed to achieve those dreams that you set for yourself when you were a prodigious little brat.

The cold was creeping in quickly. The difficult trek and subsequent climb had sustained him, but sitting still would not. He hadn't yet decided if he wanted to live through the night, but he was fairly certain he didn't want to die by hypothermia. It occurred to Dom that no one in this building would be surprised or concerned by a window breaking, but how to break it was a problem — he didn't have anything on him that could do it. The only object on the fire escape was a cheap plastic planter that had been left by the previous tenants, and which probably wouldn't leave a bruise if you smacked someone upside the head with it. There were several large rocks bordering the neighbor's garden on the ground below, but Dom wasn't sure he could get those up onto the platform, and he cringed at the thought of climbing up again. He would have to do it bare-handed.

He gave the process some thought. While he knew that punching through glass was generally a stupid thing to do, he felt like he could rapidly strike the pane and yank his hand back without sustaining any serious cuts. Still, he decided that wrapping his hand in cloth would be wise, so with some difficulty he pulled off his tattered t-shirt.

The effort didn't go quite as well as expected — the larger shards that formed at the top dropped down into his fist before he pulled back, giving him a couple of ugly stings — but the window was gone. He looked around and listened for a few seconds, but as he suspected, no lights came on, no one in the vicinity tried to investigate. He flicked a few of the remaining shards out of the window frame and carefully climbed through. For a moment he stood still, surveying the room, considering the state of his life. Dom's apartment, which he had deliberately left bare and ragged, did nothing to improve his morale. *What do I do now?* The answering machine blinked in the corner, there were three messages. *Why bother?* Dom's face strained in anguish as a chilly sadness coursed through him. By now he was too wired and pain-riddled to sleep, and again the demons permeated his thoughts. *It's over. You are over.* Tears ran down his cheeks. His face clenched as he slowly dropped to the floor, exhaling an airy, nearly-silent cry of anguish, letting all of the air leave his lungs as he curled into a ball with his head on his knees. Eyes closed, he gasped several times, trying to catch up with his sadness. Finally he regained some composure and pulled himself into a kneeling position.

His eyes glanced past the remnants of art projects in various states of completion — three old landscapes leaned against the wall, faded jeans covered a welded-steel bust sitting in the corner, drawings of all sorts lay bound in a makeshift cardboard folder on the table... *Wasted effort. Pointless wastes of energy, all of them.* He sank down again and wept into his hands. Though he wasn't sure he could bring himself to make it happen, Dom wanted to die.

He considered his options. Not having seriously considered suicide before, Dom didn't know off-hand which methods were at his disposal. Never had any reason to own a gun. Didn't own a straight razor, and wasn't sure he could cut far enough into a wrist with any of his dull kitchen knives before he passed out from the pain. Was surprised to realize there was no rope or thick cord in the apartment. Didn't think there was anything lethal in the medicine cabinet. Some other poison, perhaps? There was bleach and detergent in the closet, but Dom decided that wasn't a smart choice — the pain would be excruciating and he couldn't be sure it would actually kill him.

His eyes continued to scan the room for a few moments, then he stopped and looked down. Of course. The glass. He remembered a scene in a movie where someone died quickly and silently from a quick dagger slice across the neck. That would do nicely. He picked up one of the longer shards, grasped it firmly and slowly brought it up to his neck, still not certain of his will. His entire body was shaking. Sweat ran down his forehead, and blood was starting to well up at the base of his palm. His breathing was short, his mind was racing, and Dom was wishing he had Dr. Jack Kevorkian by his side, when... a new thought came to him. An epiphany.

✛

1994 · CARRICK HOUSEHOLD

All things considered, Eddie got along pretty well with his sister Jenna, just one year younger than he and now fighting him for the use of their mother's car. Caroline was a distant eight years old, the baby of the family and its usual court jester. At the moment she was in rare form, pretending to be a town drunk in the vein of Otis, her favorite Andy Griffith character. She had mastered a couple of the stereotypical drunkard moves but relied on overly hamming it up to keep the family's attention on her.

"I sa-, I sa-, I SAID (hic!)..." she stammered while swaying side to side, bracing herself on the edge of the dinner table. "I need THREE MORE DRINKS before I walk h-h-hooooooome, BUSTER."

Eddie was giggling, as much at her as with her. "Nah mister, yer cut-off, get outta my wax museum."

That one caught her off guard. "You-... WAX MUSEUM?!" Caroline laughed, breaking character. "I thought this was a beer bar!"

"Nope, it's a wax museum, of farm animals. That's a, uh... field rhinoceros that you're leaning on." Jenna was laying in the barcalounger, mostly just taking in the ridiculousness, while their mother Laura popped in only occasionally, otherwise prepping dinner.

"Oh my gosh," Caroline continued, turning to face the table. "I see THREE rhinoceroses! AAAAAH!" she yelled as she ran across the room, collapsing on her sister. "SHOOT IT!"

Jenna chimed in, "It's just a statue, you drunk ding-dong!"

Caroline was fake affronted. "Who you callin' a dong-ding, you dang-dung-dandellany!" Eddie snorted as he closed his eyes, shaking is head. What a clown.

"Dinner in ten, you goofballs," Paula yelled from the kitchen. That prompted Jenna to get up and take care of something in her room and the other two to wash up.

Silliness and lighthearted conversation continued as they set the table and sat down. Their father Bill had said they shouldn't wait for him, so they began digging into their food. Caroline set aside the drunk gag to alternate between eating and playing with her food. Paula questioned Jenna about a boy she had seen walking with Jenna that afternoon. "He's just a guy," Jenna responded while glancing overly away from the table.

Paula gave Eddie the side-eye. "Do you know this 'guy'?"

Eddie shrugged, disinterested. "Not really. A little." Then he noticed his sister's energy and decided to poke at it. "Oh, wait, that guy. Yeah, I think he's a drug dealer."

Jenna shot him a fierce glare. "What?! No he's not!"

"Yeah, big-time gangster," Eddie responded with a concerned expression. "That dude sells loads of Metamucil and Ibuprofen in back alleys."

His sister's face switched to pursed lips followed by a massive eye-roll. "You retard."

Caroline, who was following most of this with raised eyebrows, not catching on to Eddie's sarcasm, shrieked at that last remark. "HA! She called you-..."

"DON'T." Paula pointed her down. "That's not nice."

Caroline maintained a subtle, impish grin, looking silently at her siblings. After several quiet moments, she whispered, while staring down at her plate, "retard." Eddie and Jenna erupted in laughter while their mother covered her tightened face, trying not to laugh.

The energy dampened significantly when they heard Bill's truck crackling up the gravel driveway. Paula sighed and jumped up from the table, going to the kitchen to get his meal together. From the dining room, the kids heard their parents' voices, alternately bright and dark.

"Welcome home, darlin', how are you doing?"

"Fine."

"How was your day?"

"Fine. Tired."

"I bet you are. Let me take your coat. I've got you a plate all served up here, I'll warm it up and bring it in, why don't you go sit down."

"Yep."

Bill, always larger than life to his brood, walked in and sat down at the table, throwing an obligatory glance at all three with a single, "Hey, kids."

In unison, they all responded. "Hey daddy." Everyone sat still for the several seconds it took for Paula to finish microwaving Bill's meal.

She brought it in and set it down in front of him, being sure to throw out a quiet "Caroline, will you say grace?" before Bill had a chance to pick up a utensil. Everyone slowly bowed their heads while Caroline closed her eyes and placed her palms together and began.

"Dear Lord, we thank you for this... food and drinks and thank you for, um, our... everybody being safe, and thank you for... our house... and, um..."

"Amen," Bill interjected, glancing at her with a "that'll do" nod, then started eating. Paula glared momentarily at his down-turned head, passing a glance at the kids, then they all followed suit.

After a minute of silent eating, Laura made an effort to lighten the mood with an announcement that she had been keeping in her back pocket for this moment. "I got a call from Mrs. Johnston the art teacher today." Bill glanced her way briefly but remained aloof. She continued, "Our talented Eddie took first prize in a regional art competition!" The girls were elated.

"Whoa, no way!" exclaimed Jenna. "Was it for that sparrow drawing?"

Eddie smiled quietly and nodded. "Yeah."

"I wanna see it!" said Caroline.

"I haven't got it back yet, I'll bring it home next week."

Not wanting to kill the momentum, Laura jumped back in, "Oh! But you had a couple of new drawings you were showing me earlier, bring those out!"

Eddie hesitated just briefly, then said "okay" and went over to his backpack beside the front door. He brought back a few sheets of paper and split them up between Caroline and Jenna. The girls effused over them for a moment, then fell quiet. Jenna glanced toward their father before turning back to her dinner.

Presently, Bill was laser-focused on the chicken in front of him, maybe a bit too much, overtly disengaged from the family. Eddie was sitting to his father's left. He carelessly poked a pair of green beans with his fork and then ate them as he casually surveyed the room, then picked up one of the drawings and feigned interest in his own work for a few seconds before cautiously setting it on the table to his right, not too close to Bill but close enough to give him a view.

Casually, quietly, Eddie asked, "Dad... did you see this one?" It was a gestural ink drawing of a Native American brave, crouched behind a rock. Bill had occasionally extolled the virtues of native tribal life, and he clearly regarded them as tough, honorable people ("or at least they used to be" he once muttered under his breath).

Bill didn't talk a lot, so the family tended to pay attention when he seemed ready to. He continued processing his meal, tossing a second-long glance at Eddie's drawing before re-focusing on the food. A long moment passed with only his knife and fork striking the plate and his chewing. Finally, he said, without looking up, "You gonna make money with that?"

It was rhetorical — the implication was that he wouldn't. Eddie had nothing to say, nor did anyone else. He folded the drawing in half, transferred it to his back pocket, then proceeded to push the remaining bits of *his food around on his plate. When Bill finally put away the remainder of his meal and stood up, everyone sat just long enough to give him distance, then shifted their attention Eddie's way before he stood up as well, saying "what?" to no one in particular before leaving the room.*

It was a brisk Monday morning, three weeks after "the incident." Fall had settled in, and the Altantic winds were doing their best to herd the browning leaves of Edmund-Jones Park toward the eastern edge, where they piled against the stone base of an iron fence. The early fog and dew were fighting a losing battle with the wind and a determined sunrise. Uncountable flocks in myriad formations traveled south across a piercing yellow horizon. None of this was being recorded in the starched white pages of a Dom Winters sketch book.

Professor Johns sauntered into the studio with a notepad in one hand and a steaming mug of coffee in the other. A few of the students were touching up or hanging their pieces, but Alex and Karen were standing in the corner talking, their paintings still standing against the wall (Karen's was clearly unfinished). Johns walked over. "Hey guys. Where on earth is God's gift to art? He's starting to press his luck with these absences." Eddie had been absent as well, but no one was overly concerned about that.

They both looked distressed, Karen more than Alex. She looked out the window, lost in thought, while Alex answered, "Uh... well, he's at his apartment."

A pause hung in the air, as if Alex hoped that would be enough of an explanation, but Johns smiled and said, "And... what? Is he sick?"

Alex looked at Karen and then back at Johns. "We... don't know. He's being really cryptic, not really acknowledging... anything. I've been to his place several times and all I can get is a couple of words out of him. He won't open the door."

Johns was no longer smiling. "Drugs?"

Alex took a deep breath and said, "Normally I'd say no way, but we just have no idea. Except that depression is probably part of it. I assume you heard about the accident."

"Of course," Johns said, and looked down. "Everyone did. I assume that was a shock to Dom."

Karen finally chimed in. "You could say that. He was catatonic for about twenty minutes after it happened. I couldn't get him..." She brushed a tear away. "I couldn't get him to say anything until the medics tried to take him away. Even then he would just stare into space and talk to nobody in particular, like he was lobotomized or something."

"And he's been exactly like that ever since," Alex said. "I haven't been able to get a real conversation out of him, and... well, you know as much as we do at this point."

Johns pursed his lips. "Right. Okay, well, we're going over there — all of us. Either he needs our help or he owes us an explanation."

Dom's apartment building neatly fit the starving artist mold: all function and no form, not a redeeming trait other than the open spaces it afforded its occupants. Not as gruff-looking as Dom and therefore less intimidating, Alex never quite felt comfortable in this down-trodden neighborhood that was home to odd-job-seekers, beggars, addicts and the occasional thug. Johns was a native, however, and his casual stride made clear to anyone watching that he felt as safe here as anywhere. Karen stuck close to him. Alex kept his head down and led the way into the building.

Dom's loft was at the back of the second floor. Two dingy brass dead-bolts secured the heavy door, and the scratches and chips revealing multiple repaintings illustrated the need for them. Johns knocked firmly below the peep hole and they waited several seconds in silence.

He knocked again. "Dom? You there?" Another short wait, and then a third series of knocks. "Dom, it's Evan. Please open the door." Still no response. "Dom, we're not going to leave. We want to know what's going on." Nothing.

"Maybe he actually went out," Alex finally said.

Johns glanced sideways at him. "I don't think you actually believe that." He looked at Karen, who shook her head slowly in agreement.

Again he turned to the door and knocked, a bit more firmly, waited a few seconds and knocked again, then was about to knock a fourth time when they heard a faint clatter inside. Karen yelled, "Dom, open the damn door!" She looked a bit surprised after she said it.

Footsteps approached. The locks were quickly thrown open and the door swung a few inches inward to reveal a sweaty Dom, slightly out of breath and even more dishevelled than usual, with a healing black eye and bruises on his chin and collarbone. He stared at them for a few seconds and said without emotion, "What?"

Alex and Karen were mostly taken aback, but Johns only showed concern. "How are you, Dom?" he asked quietly.

The answer was immediate and still emotionless: "Fine." Quick glances again at the other two, then finally a bit of surprise mixed with irritation. "I'm *fine*."

He started to close the door on them, but Johns quickly reached out and pushed it open again. "Whoa, whoa. Dom, come on. Do you really think we'd show up just to hear you say you're fine and then leave? You don't look fine. Tell us what's going on with you."

Dom stared evenly at Johns for several seconds. He seemed to be having difficulty caring about the current situation. "I'm working."

John's eyebrows raised slowly. "Working!" He squinted his eyes in a skeptical look. "Really?"

"Yeah. Really." Still staring.

A long pause. Johns was trying, as he tended to do, to let his student snap out of his impolite silence and start communicating, but Dom was the most hard-headed of students, and he wasn't budging. "Then... may we see what you're working on?"

Dom's face quickly snapped from cool neutrality to surprised indignation, as though he hadn't even considered such a ridiculous option. His mind was still not fully engaged in the situation.

He stared like this a moment longer, then glanced at each of them in turn a couple of times, as though he were considering his options. Finally he raised his arm, limply pointed at Alex and said, "You," as though they had never met. He stepped back and pulled the door open a few more inches. Alex threw a bewildered glance at the other two and stepped gingerly inside. The door shut firmly behind him and one of the locks snapped shut.

It is the nature of artists not to care one whit about the neatness of their living space. If they were capable of keeping their rooms clean then they'd probably be just as happy in graphic design or architecture, where they would be more likely to get paid. Dom was nothing special in this vein, he was as messy as the next art geek, but the current state of his loft broke new ground in the world of slovenliness. The motif appeared to be "ode to the picked-at take-out dinner." Chow mein containers, pizza boxes, burger wrappers, Coke cans and beer bottles had been crammed into every available corner after the overflowing garbage can had supported its last food remnant. The flies were so pleased.

Whatever surfaces weren't covered by that mess were used to support sketches, hundreds of them. Some of these were thrown to the floor, torn asunder where they met with walking paths. Some (assumedly these were sketches) were in wads near the garbage heap. Many were tacked up on top of one another, hanging from walls, each sketch

45

more detailed and carefully rendered than the one before it. All of them depicted what looked to Alex like a chair that was bolstered with some sort of apparatus behind, underneath, above or around it. All of the more developed images featured a large spring.

Alex was so mesmerized by the food and sketch parade that he hadn't noticed a new array of heavy power tools sitting on the workbench in the back. "When did you get all of those?"

"Hm? Uh... couple weeks ago. Mail order." Dom was focused on the spring apparatus of one of the larger sketches.

Also thus far unnoticed, partly because it was covered in the same dingy gray canvas that all of Dom's furniture (to use the term loosely) was usually covered in, was a fairly large object in the middle of the room. It was evident from the shape that this was a real-life version of what had been so diligently mastered on paper. Dom finally took his eyes off one of the sketches long enough to see that Alex had noticed the object. He walked over to it and reached his hand toward the cover but stopped short of pulling it off.

"Um..." His hand dropped back to his side. "So I guess I've been... kind of gone for awhile," he said, now more focused and able to carry on a normal conversation. Alex smiled slightly and nodded. Dom considered his words for a moment. "I... went down a dark road there, after the accident at the Hole. Things were... bad. In my mind. I just... between school, and art, and Eddie... I couldn't cope." He was staring at the canvas, almost mumbling. "Somebody kicked the shit out of me, outside a bar. I couldn't think straight. I was in a lot of pain. I, um... I couldn't cope. Anymore."

Alex was listening intently. Not a sound could be heard between Dom's strained words. Dom seemed now to at least be focused on the story he was telling.

"Well, it's kind of hard to talk about." He reached out again and grabbed a handful of canvas. "Maybe this will fill in the blanks." The corner of his mouth twisted into a slight grin as he carefully pulled back the cover and dropped it on the floor.

Alex never had the mastery of mechanics that came easily to Dom, so it took a few minutes of staring at the oddly-shaped chair in front of him to connect the dots. It appeared to be a chair whose wooden back was a wide, flat slab interrupted at the center by a large round hole, and hanging diagonally downward from either side were two flat planks that pointed at the ground, appearing to support nothing. But the heavy hinge joining the back and seat made it clear that these appendages would in fact support arms once the occupant leaned backward, where...

A pair of narrow metal triangles had been welded together to form a single spike pointing up from the floor behind the chair's back. A tall, coiled spring that enclosed the spike was anchored at its top to a horizontal board the same length as the chair back, the board offering a wide hole to the spike/spring apparatus, in just the same spot as the hole in the chair back. Alex mentally pushed the back of the chair down onto the horizontal board and realized what was supposed to happen next. His eyes widened and his jaw went slack.

Uneasily, he spoke. "Oh, shit..." Eventually he took his eyes off of the chair to look at its creator, who was grinning and eyeing the object with a mix of lust and pride that matched Alex's fright and confusion.

"You know what it is, right?" Dom said without taking his eyes away from it.

Alex said quietly, "I know what it looks like, Dom."

"It *is* what it looks like," Dom said, his grin widening. He glanced up and did a double-take at the look on Alex's face and said, "Oh, I'm not going to *use* it!"

"You're not?"

The grin returned, this time mockingly, "No, no — it's just a piece, Alex!" Alex didn't look convinced. "Oh, well... sure, the..." His grin faded and he looked down. "...inspiration for it was real enough." He reached up and scratched his forehead. "I couldn't cope with it all, you know? I didn't... I was..."

He was staring away, into space. "Well, that's..." He looked tired and distraught. "That's what it took, Alex. That's what it finally took. To find the inspiration."

Tears were welling in his eyes as he finally looked up and smiled slightly. "I found it, Lex." His face was an even mix of happy and sad. "I found it."

peaks

"Jesus Christ."

Reactions around the room varied from disgust to amusement, but were dominated by uneasiness and fear. Dom could barely contain his giddiness. *The Conclusion* sat on a clean white slab at the center of its own large gallery space, separated from the crowd by black felt ropes.

"The thing that I love the most about this piece is that you don't have to explain the concept to anyone, whether they're in the art world or not. Even if they can't describe in words what the core concept is or why it works, it visibly affects them." Dom radiated with an even mixture of excitement and arrogance. "If you sit on that bench and look at the expressions of people who walk in, you can tell that it disturbs most of them, and yet they can't *not* look at it — the danger is too captivating."

The reporter raised his eyebrows. "If I didn't know any better I'd swear you're feeding off of their fear."

"Oh, not as such. I just enjoy the power of the reaction. That's what art is all about — drawing emotion out of people, compelling them to feel something. This is not a Norman Rockwell sculpture, Chris. The chair is a dark, deadly thing, and only because it actually works."

"You've tested it, then?"

Dom closed his eyes and shook his head slightly in an arrogant you-silly-underling expression. "Never. It just isn't necessary — the mechanism is too simple not to work. I feel like it would degrade the impact of the thing to actually test it. The fact that the hammer has never been thrown adds to the intrigue."

Alex had been lingering nearby, but decided to wander outside for some fresh air. He had voluntarily accepted an unofficial position as Dom's assistant, partly because he wanted to support Dom in his ascension to fame, but also because the cliff incident and resulting events had left him with an uneasy feeling about Dom's emotional stability.

Alex pulled out a cigarette and hung it on his lips, unlit. He had been doing a good job kicking the habit, but he still felt the need to go through the motions. He had some time to kill, so he bought a paper from the USA Today machine. There were two *Conclusion* mentions inside: a short second-page story about a mother-driven protest group in some Wisconsin suburb and an editorial cartoon in the opinion section wherein a disgruntled wife replaced her husband's recliner with a *Conclusion*-style chair.

The chair was one of the current "big things" in the public eye at that point and all sorts of media were referencing it in one way or another — regional point/counterpoint talk shows debated Dom's ethics and purpose, bloggers and other web denizens analyzed the apparatus itself from every conceivable angle, journalists gathered what data they could about Dom's past (as well as the outbursts and episodes that preceded the chair's unveiling by just a few months). And then of course there were the comedians...

"Ladies and gentleman, my next guest is a successful young artist and the creator of the controversial 'suicide chair,' which recently graced the cover of Time Magazine. Please welcome Dominic Winters!"

Dominic walked out from the stage-left curtain in what had become his standard uniform: black slacks, black blazer, black button-up shirt with pastel buttons. With only some gel and a few adjustments, his hair had conveniently fallen into the unkempt style currently worn by the trendiest male celebs. He also wore his now standard chipper/confident grin and walk. One of the rare Letterman guests who topped the host in height, he accommodatingly bowed a bit as he shook Dave's hand before sitting down.

"So Dom... you go by Dom, right?"

Dom nodded his head. "Yes, only my artwork calls me Dominic."

"Right." Dave chuckled. "You're keeping really busy these days, I take it."

Dom smiled. "Yeah, you might say that — my life has really turned on its head since the chair's unveiling. I'm actually flying to San Francisco in an hour and have to be back here again tomorrow morning."

"An hour you say, so... that must be a red-eye flight," Dave said as he flashed a patronizing grin at the afternoon audience. He got his laugh and turned back to his guest. "Man, that's rough. So I'm guessing you don't have much time to work on your art right now, do you?"

"Hardly any, my schedule is packed with this type of thing." Dom had clearly gotten used to the publicity, but of course he had been dreaming about it since he was a teenager. "Some promotional work is expected in an artist's life, but this thing has kind of gotten out of hand. I feel like I just wrote a bestseller or something."

Paul Shaffer chimed in. "You sculpted one."

Dave: "Yeah, in a way you sculpted a bestseller."

"Yep, that's true." Dom always preferred non-art-world interviews like these — he had never enjoyed the stilted verbiage used in art magazines and analytical books.

"And is this the sort of artwork that you normally create?"

"Well, not necessarily — certainly I've never created an... instrument of death before," chuckles from the audience. "I've never really pinned myself down to a particular medium, but these days I create industrial sculptures more than anything else."

"Uh-huh," Dave said. "It's, uh... it's really bothering some people, this chair-"

"Yeah, some people don't like it, and I knew that would be the case before I started building it." Dom crossed his legs. "But I would be remiss not to work with a concept just because it was controversial."

"Well, I couldn't agree more, that's why we're so cutting-edge here at the Late Show." Dave threw his trademark grin/pause at the camera and waited for another laugh before turning back to Dom. "So tell me in your own words why this thing is such a big deal."

Dom looked away into space and brought his fingertips together, as though he was about to drop some knowledge on America. "Well, I think that it's shocking in its directness. Any number of artistic works could be used to commit suicide, but until now none have been created to... announce their purpose so boldly." Dom turned back to Dave with a slight smile on his lips. "There's nothing subtle about *The Conclusion*."

Dave grinned back just before a photo of the piece was shown on the screen. "No, absolutely not. Now, how... and I realize this must be a touchy subject for you, but I'm compelled to ask. How did you come up with the idea for the piece, what was the inspiration?"

"Of course." Dom pursed his lips for a moment, then delivered his standard half-true explanation. "Well, everyone has their ups and downs, you know — things can pile up on you in a way that can make life seem impossibly painful. I myself was in the middle of a down period when I happened to catch a segment on the news about Jack Kevorkian-"

Dave interjected, "And that cheered you right up I bet." Dom and the audience chuckled.

"Yeah, he's a ray of sunshine," his smile tapered off and he continued. "I am a big supporter of what he's done, of course, but I decided that I wanted to create something that would send you off — if you so choose — not in a gentle, painless fashion but a heavy, jarring one, a dramatic death that, in an intense sort of way, celebrates life by immediately activating everything in your body that gives you your life, just before taking it away. With *The Conclusion* I strove for boldest, simplest kind of death."

Dave stared at Dom in silence for a few seconds, then turned to Paul. "Who the hell booked this guy?" Laughter all around.

Blistering sunshine rained down on the idyllic Sunset Strip. A light breeze tussled Robert Redford's golden locks while a parade of expensive sports cars ambled past the front of the stylish open-air cafe where he and Dom had ordered brunch. It was an epically California moment.

The small talk and gratuitous *Conclusion* questions were over, and Mr. Redford had rolled almost without pause into his primary mission: commissioning Dom for a flagship installation at the upscale gallery he would be launching the following year in Santa Barbara. The legendary actor was known almost as well in Southern California for his art scholarship, and he had studied up on Dom's history after the chair landed in headlines everywhere. It went without saying that Mr. Redford wasn't bothered by the edgy nature of Dom's masterwork. The request was equal parts exciting and flattering, but Dom was having trouble concentrating on the conversation, chomping at the bit to ask about the Paul Newman glory days.

"I'd like to get you out to the site sometime soon. But for now, here are some photos of the space." Redford handed Dom a stack of professionally-shot 8x10s with one hand while sipping his amusingly frilly coffee drink with the other. "Rachel Whiteread already called dibs on the atrium, but you're welcome to select the entryway or any of the other spaces. It's not the MOMA, but we've got about 6000 square feet of beautiful floor space."

Dom nodded, trying not to look too impressed with the strikingly designed building he was seeing — this was a business meeting, after all. "It's... really great," he said with a casual smile. "I would love the opportunity to develop a piece for the gallery." In his peripheral vision he noticed something with bouncing blond pigtails approaching rapidly from the other side of the street.

"Terrific. Then let's have you fly back out to this coast in a few..." Redford began, but Dom's attention was diverted to the approaching teenager, long enough to spot the pen and pad in her hands. He grinned and turned his attention to his soup. Redford's sentence trailed off just as the girl appeared and spoke up.

"I'm so sorry to bother you, but could I get your autograph?" A silent pause followed. Dom wiped his mouth with his napkin and accommodatingly glanced around at other tables, biding his time, before his eyes landed on Redford, who was staring back at Dom with the trademark pearly white grin, not signing his name. Dom then looked up at the girl, who was offering her book and pen not to the Sundance Kid, but to the famous sculptor.

Just ten months after the chair's unveiling, the Library of Congress issued a grant for a suite of official archival data on *The Conclusion* to be created. Veteran photographer Andrew Silver and author May Williams were contracted for the job, and a date was set for Dom to be interviewed and present to them any and all historical materials (mock-ups, sketches, notes, tools, and environments) that went into the conception and creation of the chair. Dom would meet them at the Fizi Gallery in Boston where the chair was on display, then proceed to his former digs near the Cape Johns art campus, which had since been taken over by another grad student but were in more or less the same condition that Dom had left them.

It was necessary before all of this took place for *The Conclusion* to undergo a detailed cleaning, a job which Dom refused to grant to anyone but himself. He arrived in his old t-shirt and jeans (which was refreshing after five weeks of formal shirts and starched suits) at the gallery early in the morning, four hours prior to the event, carrying a large duffel bag that contained a litany of brushes, sponges, polishers and solvents. He rounded the corner of the chair's space and smiled at his creation. "Good morning, beautiful!"

It was a labor of love, but it was a labor indeed, and Dom was glad that he had allotted so much time to the task. Polishing the object was more than a little bit akin to polishing his own ego, and a great deal of elbow grease went into making sure *The Conclusion* appeared to be fresh off the factory floor, gleaming where it ought to gleam and soaking up the light where it ought to be deathly black. It was so pristine that one would almost forget about the gruesome torment that it was ever ready to unleash.

Dom whistled while he worked. He was rubbing in steady backwards circles with a cotton diaper that had been dipped in a bowl of diluted

Pledge when he brushed a hair too close to the hole at the top of the spring and heard a faint click. He would never be sure which sensation he experienced first — the thunderous, metallic bang that echoed through the gallery halls as the spike's restricting collar struck the chair base, or the searing sting in the side of his forearm where the spike's needle tip ripped through his skin, just missing his ulna. *The Conclusion's* hammer had fired for the first time.

Dom screamed and collapsed backward in shock, momentarily transfixed by the still-vibrating, blood-streaked cone that jutted into the air in front of him. The raw, precise power of the mechanism, which had previously been just a daydream for Dom, had now made its presence felt in the most unmistakable terms. Pain hadn't yet caught up with fear when he surveyed the surrounding hallways and listened silently for footsteps. Apparently no one had been within earshot.

He regained himself, wrapped and tied the last clean diaper he had around his arm, then called Alex on his cell. "Lex. I, uh... had an accident. I need you to bring the compression rig and a first-aid kit to the gallery. *Now.*" Alex arrived twenty minutes later, and the pair spent the last hour feverishly erasing all evidence of what had happened, then getting the artist cleaned and primped for his private show. No doubt this would someday make a juicy entry in the annals that Dom was preparing to help write, but no one was going to hear this story until the artist was ready to tell it.

depths

"Sit, please."

There are those moments in life when a short pause in conversation feels deathly pregnant and stretches on forever, when you fear the worst but pray for the best, hope beyond hope that your heart is beating out of your chest for nothing, that whatever 'this' is turns out to be tiny instead of devastating. Eve could tell that something was up the minute she walked in the door, when Barbara asked Eve to sit instead of greeting her with a kiss and a grope. Barb was still her boss, of course, and it would make sense to switch over to business mode if there was something job-related to discuss — a botched communication with a client, an obliviously offensive remark in the kitchen, something about the tchotchkes on Eve's desk... who knows.

That was the hope, the prayer. Anything confined to the job and not about the relationship. Barb glanced for a moment out the window of her nature-facing office, then back at Eve briefly before averting her gaze to her desk instead. Eve's concern and heart rate grew with every second of silence. This was not normal. She could feel herself buzzing by the time she finally, after too much silence had passed, asked in a clipped, strained manner, "What?"

Barb looked up and stared at Eve with resolve and forced composure. "It's over."

No. Not those words. They landed like gunshots. She could barely breath, could barely hold it together enough to repeat, this time with a different meaning, "What?"

Barb was silent for another moment. "We won't be seeing each other anymore."

Tears were welling in Eve's eyes. She began to tremble. "No." Her head shook side to side. "No. Don't. Please, Barb. My love."

Barbara responded almost robotically. "I'm sorry, but things have chang-"

"WHAT things?" Eve shot back.

Barb paused, alternately staring at Eve and the desk, before reaching down to a side table and transferring a box of tissues to the edge of the desk in front of Eve, who ignored it, pleading with despondent eyes while tears streamed down her face.

"I won't be leaving Thomas."

Eve's eyebrows lifted in shock. The floor seemed to drop out from under her. In the four years they had been secretly dating, Barb had scarcely offered a complimentary word about her husband, who she was positive was having at least the third affair of their nineteen year marriage. As far as Eve had ever known, Bobby was the definition of a crass, soulless, entitled waste of space, and it had long been understood that Barb was only putting in hard time to reach a prenup milestone that would allow her to take her husband to the cleaners in a divorce. It was all very clearly laid out, down to the day she would hand him the papers. Not once had Barb wavered in this plan. Not once in four years.

Several empty seconds passed while Eve struggled to comprehend what was happening, now staring blankly into space. Finally, she asked, without returning her gaze to Barb, "Why?"

The answer was so immediate that it felt rehearsed, and unnecessarily harsh: "It doesn't matter." Eve shot a glance sideways at her, startled. Barb felt slightly embarrassed by the tone and relented a bit. "Sorry. It's just... it doesn't matter. And the decision is final."

Eve's universe was falling apart. She couldn't even properly cry, she simply slipped into a catatonic state. She could barely breathe.

Barb's face hinted at her burgeoning desire to end the conversation and part ways. Yet another silent minute passed before she felt the need to move things along. "I'd like for you to leave now." The words barely registered. Eve slowly directed her eyes over to Barb, making sure she understood what had just been requested. Barb stoically returned the glance and added, "Please."

Nearly immobilized by shock, Eve had just enough control of her faculties to compel her body to move. She leaned forward in her chair, everything about it and her movements feeling unnatural. Awkwardly, she pushed against the toe of her pumps and turned out of the chair, resting much of her weight on the chair's arm in a struggle to stand.

Still not sufficiently breathing, vision obscured by tears and barely in control of her motor function, Eve's next step faltered and she fell to the floor.

"Oh, for the love of-... get it together, Evelyn." This crossed a line for Barb, rapidly losing patience with the drama of the moment and concerned that it could further snowball. She paused for a moment after the remark, hoping that Eve would stand back up on her own, but begrudgingly rose from behind her desk and walked over to assist. She could hear the hiss of Eve's distraught, whimpering breath as tears one by one fell to the burnt orange carpet. While she didn't want physical contact to add to the emotional intensity, she desperately needed for this to be over, so she leaned down to grasp Eve's wrists and lift her upright. "Stand, Eve. Come on, stand up."

Eve allowed herself to be lifted. "I'm sorry," she whispered, internally surprised she was apologizing. But she couldn't imagine emotionally standing firm when she couldn't physically stand on her own.

"It's fine. I get that it's hard." Barb thought maybe a modicum of empathy would ease the tension. She let go of Eve's wrists, but Eve's arms still hung for a few seconds in space. Eve's mascara was forming trails down both cheeks, and Barb pulled a tissue from the box on her desk and gently but briskly wiped them. Barb silently took a deep breath. "Okay, so. Can you... do you think you can make it home?"

She was putting on a "kind" demeanor, but the effort felt hollow on both ends.

Barb had obviously timed this announcement for the end of a Friday so that it wouldn't look out of place for Eve to go straight home afterward. Even still, this was a worrying situation — she didn't anticipate the conversation being easy, but she wasn't prepared for Eve to be so utterly leveled. Eve really was trying, it was all she could do to put one foot in front of the other. Without saying a word, she hobbled toward the door, which Barb walked to and opened for her.

Eve's pace picked up slightly, but otherwise failed to improve after walking into the cubicle farm. Instead of turning into her own cubicle to retrieve her jacket, purse and lunch bag, she continued down the walkway, heading straight for the elevator. Few people were still in the office, but Mark, one of Eve's buddies from the marketing department, noticed her with a double-take.

"Hey there, punk-... Eve? Eve. What's wrong?" She paid no notice, continuing her path to the elevator button. His words and her behavior caught the attention of two other employees who were getting ready to leave. "EVE," he tried once more before the elevator doors finally opened and Eve walked in, slowly turned, pushed a button, then remained facing the corner of the elevator with a blank stare.

Twenty yards away, peering through her half-closed office door, Barb watched the scene unfold with increasing discomfort. After the elevator doors closed, Mark looked back at Barb's office and caught her leering. For two seconds they locked eyes before Barb turned away and abruptly shut the door.

Mark didn't know what to make of what just happened, though he guessed that Eve had been canned. Why? He hadn't seen or heard about anything specific that would get her fired, but... she had always been a bit of a wild card, and he couldn't know all of her activity at the company. Mark wasn't sure what to do, but Eve was his friend, he needed to do something. He looked around his own desk absentmindedly before walking over to Eve's. It did not look like the scene of an employee who has gone home, much less one who is gone forever. He looked around the office, which was otherwise vacated, then over at Barb's closed door. Probably not the time to knock, that glare had scared the hell out of him.

He surveyed the desk again before starting with the obvious: putting her computer to sleep. He put his hand on the mouse then paused for a moment, considering poking around for evidence of what was going on, but immediately thought better of it and logged her out. All that was left was to deal with her belongings. Again, he looked around — it was a little weird for a man to be taking possession of a female coworker's things. He was about to pick up the purse but decided to try calling her first, pulling out his phone and tapping her name only to realize immediately afterward that her phone was in the purse, blaring a tinny electronic rendition of Missy Elliott's 'Get Ur Freak On.' He ended the call and paused, trying to figure out his next move. Even if Eve was headed straight home (hopefully she was), she probably wouldn't have gotten there yet, but Mark decided to try her land line anyway. His finger halted above the Call button when Barb's door opened.

After abruptly shutting the door on Mark, Barb was near panic, an unusual state for her. Eve's overtly devastated behavior had already thrown her plan out of whack, but her zombie exit threw the situation into complete chaos. No one could know about their relationship, that would be catastrophic for Barb's financial future. Granted, Eve's recent behavior had essentially forced Barb's hand. But that didn't diminish the current danger. "What the fuck," she whispered to herself. "What the fucking *fuck* do I do here?"

She took a deep breath and walked back to her desk and sat down, staring absently into her desk. Barb knew that time was of the essence, but she didn't want to take actions haphazardly or dig herself into a deeper hole. She looked for logical explanations for the situation from the top down:

› Eve acted shell-shocked. Why: because she's been fired.

› Why she was fired: she's been trying to create a relationship with Barb for years — flirting, stalking, threatening. That's believable, people will believe she would do that. Will Mark believe it? Maybe. Probably.

› So, she's been fired, what does that mean? She needs to be locked out of all office systems, immediately: electronic locks, computer, email, voice mail, etc. Barb has always retained access to those systems alongside the HR, IT and security staff.

› Then what? Eve will deny the accusation, obviously. Barb's word against hers, which will work on everyone except... her husband, Bobby. Whether or not Eve has any proof, that fucker will know.

› So... soooooo... Shit. What. What the hell was she supposed to do, have Eve *commit-*...?

Barb paused. Son of a bitch. Could that work? It might. But again — time. She had to act.

Jumping up and rounding the corner of her desk so fast that she nearly tore her skirt on the corner, Barb ran to the door and pulled it open, careful to slow her movement at the last moment to ensure it didn't seem rushed on the other side. He was still there.

Again, they locked eyes momentarily. "Mark, hi. Can I... talk with you for a minute?"

Barb was unusually warm — she waved him to one of the two chairs in front of her desk then sat in the other. "I suppose you're wondering what happened with-," she stopped. "I'm sorry, would you like a glass of water or anything?"

Mark was off-balance, this moment was completely weird. "Hm? Oh, no. No, I'm... fine, thank you."

"Okay, sorry. Anyway," she continued, "you're probably wondering what that was all about." She tilted her head toward the door. "I'll admit I wasn't sure what to expect from her." Always mix a bit of truth into subterfuge. She glanced up at Mark to gauge where he was at. His face was mostly blank, with a hint of fear. She decided to back up a bit, both for intel and to create connection. "How well do you know Eve?"

Mark awkwardly nodded, then said, "Ah, yeah. We're... pretty good friends. Mostly here at the office, but we're... friends outside of the office, too. We hang out sometimes."

"Sure," Barb nodded back. Pretty much what she already knew, since Eve had suggested as much. She was also fairly certain that Mark new nothing more about their relationship — Eve cared enough about it to swear up and down that she had diligently kept it to herself. But still... "So, just out of curiosity, did she ever mention a... a *relationship*," sidelong glance, "with me?"

Mark's perplexed reaction confirmed her expectations. He was no actor, and that question took him by surprise. "Relationship? No, she never said anything like that."

That response locked in Barb's plan. If Mark hadn't already been told that she and Eve were dating, there was no reason to hold back. She took a breath and continued.

"Okay. Well, there *wasn't* one," she said in a frank and direct tone. "However. Eve... Jesus, where to begin." This was all the prelude for a woman who had years of experience diving into stories based on half-truths. "Eve wanted a relationship with me. For years. And eventually," she sighed. "Eventually she believed there *was* one, she just... invented more and more delusion around it. Our *business* relationship never changed, but her... her perception of it did." A pause to look toward the window and exude sadness. "I do care about Eve, Mark. But we never had any kind of a relationship other than what you saw in this office."

Still a blank expression. "Okay."

She pressed on. "For most of that time, her behavior was only a minor nuisance — a flirty remark here, a suggestive birthday card there... it wasn't frequent enough to piss me off, even after I realized that she was serious. I guess she was playing the long game." A pause for effect, and to start including parts of the story that were actually true. "That changed... about two weeks ago. She suddenly started calling me at odd hours — dinner time, bed time. Then she showed up at my home last Saturday. I'm not even sure how she got the address, but I guess that isn't top secret info." Mark's eyes had gotten wider by this point, his face more concerned. "I found her chatting with my daughter in the driveway. Stacy isn't old enough to recognize the shock on my face, but my husband Bobby would have if I hadn't had a few seconds to compose myself before he heard the chatter and came outside. I played it off — she is a coworker, after all — and politely told her goodbye, but... that was the last straw, Mark. I was shocked and terrified."

"Oh my god." Mark leaned forward and placed his face in his hands. "I can't believe it. I mean, I guess I *can*, it's just..."

"Well, for that matter, I don't guess there's any proof, so I would understand if you didn't believe me," Barb said, cementing the opposite feeling into place with false humility.

"Oh, no no, Mrs. Green," Mark jumped in, "I believe you. As shocking as it is to hear all this..." He struggled with his words and half shrugged. "I... I guess I can kind of imagine her doing that stuff."

"Yeah. She's not exactly a shrinking violet around here," she said with a quiet smile, simultaneously realizing that she would need more ammo in order to reach her true objective. She took a deep breath and stared intently at Mark. "There's more."

Eve was on autopilot. Between the office lobby and her apartment building doorstep she had mustered conscious thought only enough to operate doors and her legs. Every few people who crossed her path gave her a double-take or a concerned check-in — all met with zero response. That same minuscule awareness was called upon at Eve's apartment door, where she, having left her purse on her desk, realized that she required the spare key that she kept in a sealed pocket buried in the side of a potted plant in the building's garden. Eve navigated the path back to her doorway as a robot. The hallways were mostly empty this time of day, but she was able to mutter a quiet "hi" to her upstairs neighbor Agnes who greeted Eve when she reached her floor.

She stepped inside and turned to close the door, every motion feeling awkward and meaningless, and almost required basic commands in her mind — 'remove the key from the lock; now close the door; lock it behind you; remember to breathe; now probably turn around.' She turned. Now what? She felt the metal key in her hand and glanced around the room, not really registering anything more than the familiarity of her space. It felt oppressively quiet and stagnant. Flashes of moments here with Barb popped in but didn't linger, her system wasn't open to that yet. She stood still with no tangible thought for the next five minutes, eyes wandering listlessly, slowly breathing, moisture forming inside the key-holding hand.

Finally, she succumbed to the need to change position, walking forward past her tiny kitchen (dropping the sweaty key on her counter) and into the "living room." Again she gazed around her, feebly looking for inspiration. Cloudy afternoon sun floated through the blinds, evenly lighting the largely white-leaning decor of her apartment. Kids laughed in the distance, followed by an ambulance siren even farther. She glanced at the TV and DVD player. Maybe she should watch a movie. Maybe read her book. Maybe take a nap? Those are things people do.

She sat on the loveseat. Another brief Barb memory flash, Barb going down on her the night they caught Donnie Darko and dinner on the other side of town. It went away again, she stared at her little component stereo. She didn't even entertain the idea of getting up and putting music on. Her gaze softened as her mind fell back into floating emptiness. 45 minutes passed with barely a thought or movement other than an occasional deep breath. She was hungry, and needed to pee, but not enough to move.

Evening arrived another hour later and it finally became critical to get up and relieve herself. Slowly she leaned forward, looked at the floor, then at the arm of the loveseat, carefully placing her hand on it before struggling to a standing position. She paused momentarily before turning toward the bathroom and hobbling toward it.

Sitting on the toilet, staring out the bathroom doorway at the wall beyond, Eve considered getting her bottle of tequila out from its hiding place under the sink, surprised that idea hadn't come to her until now. No point hiding that anymore. No one around to take it out of her hands and pour it down the drain, to pull the antidepressant contraindication warnings up on the web and recite what Eve obviously already knew, *duh*.

Fuck her. Still sitting on the toilet, Eve opened the cabinet, reached down to grab the down-facing bottle behind cleaning supplies, knocked over a bottle of Windex pulling it out, and without so much as glancing at it, unscrewed the cap and guzzled half of the half bottle that was left. Now *that* felt like something, the toxic sensation coating her throat, breaking through her stupor. She took another swig, re-capped the bottle, and stood up.

Eve returned to the living room, now dimming in the evening light, looked around again, then... collapsed to the floor and began sobbing, all of the heartache landsliding across her shoulders. Memories now came at her in a torrent: weekend trips to the islands; carefully secreted make-outs in Barb's office; their road trip through New England last fall; kisses, sex and intimate conversations in every corner of Eve's apartment. Magic, all of it. Always curtailed by the limits of conceal-ment, but that usually made it hotter and more fun, and it was always paired with the promise and vision of a post-Bobby future together. They discussed that future regularly, both of them pining for it, holding it as the long-term prize for their loving patience, cradling it as the lifeblood of their existence.

Eve cried out in pain. Gone. All of that, gone, forever. No more vision. No more moments. No more Barb and Eve. No more Barb.

Mark let the air out of his lungs and dropped his face into his hands, his fingers sliding through the front locks of his hair. "Oh my god."

"Yeah. That's what I said to myself." By this point Barb had moved to a standing position near the window, gazing absentmindedly at the horizon. "It brought me to tears, Mark. I've never been in this kind of situation before."

Barb had doubled down on Mark's trust by diving into an emotional half-yarn about Eve catching Barb's eye through the bathroom window of Barb's house late at night, her eyes red from crying. She nearly added a bit about Eve raising a knife to her own neck, but stopped herself, realizing that might be going a notch too far. The irony was that Barb could have told more *true* stories in support of the "crazy Eve" case, but they all would expose the romantic relationship. She hoped she hadn't added any details to this version that would come back to bite her later. Still, she had to press on...

"I'm... just not sure what to do now. I really worry that Eve is going to hurt herself. Or me. Or my family." She looked up at him, willing him to suggest it. "You saw what she looked like earlier. She was... just totally despondent."

Mark was fully off-kilter, he looked ill. "Well, yeah... I don't know — maybe... she needs to be in a hospital or something?"

Barb lightly nodded, gazing downward. "Yeah, I guess that would seem to make sense. Though... it's hard to imagine either of us convincing her to do that." She looked up again. "And if she ran..."

Mark's shoulders slumped. "Yeah. Right."

A long pause ensued. Barb decided she had probably built enough support.

"I do actually know a psychiatrist — I wonder if we shouldn't ask him about this."

Mark's eyebrows lifted. "Oh! Yeah." His tone adjusted back downward. "That... seems like a good idea."

Barb's "friend" Kyle was actually her husband Bobby's sidekick, and while he was a psychiatrist, he was also of similar ethical caliber. She knew she would only have to throw a subtle hint or two Kyle's way and he would read between the lines: Barb needed this person out of the way.

After coercing Mark's buy-in on the committal plan, Barb suggested that they call Kyle on speakerphone, but she first wanted to text him to make sure he would be available for a call so late (as well as include an important clue: "worth your while"). Kyle responded yes, call away.

Normally Kyle's delivery would have tended toward the brash end, even while interfacing with a professional woman, but he shrewdly began the call wielding his most doctoral tone. "Great to hear from you, Barb, though I gather under not very pleasant circumstances."

"Yes, I'm afraid not, Dr. Bandon." She had never once called him that. "We're kind of at our wits' end," she added while making eye contact with Mark. "I really hate calling on you so late, but we feel like time is of the essence here, our friend may be a danger to herself. Or others."

The conversation went almost exactly as Barb wanted, save for a lack of proactive participation on Mark's part — while he was head-nodding to everything being recounted and theorized, including background about Eve's behavior and personality, he only volunteered his own contributions when asked. Still, Kyle made up for Mark's inertia with deftly leading questions that gave Mark no choice but to support the argument that Eve was simply too unstable to be left to her own devices.

"Okay. Well." The case seemed to have been laid to rest, and an uncomfortable pause settled on the call. Barb looked again over at Mark. "Kyle, what are your thoughts?"

Kyle smartly paused for a few seconds before answering. "I just don't see any way around it, guys — she needs to be in a hospital. Frankly, it would be irresponsible for me not to press for that."

Thus it was settled, and the remainder of the call dealt with logistics: securing a court order, an ambulance, a couple of strong nurses, and a police officer; making contact with Eve's building manager; notifying the psychiatric hospital that Kyle was affiliated with about the incoming patient; and a brief discussion of insurance benefits that likely covered such hospitalization, to be more fully explored once the "crisis" was abated. The "rescue team" agreed to meet at an all-night diner near Eve's apartment, then proceed on foot to her door. Mark was visibly freaked out, and despite her resolve to make this happen, Barb was also fairly uneasy. It's not every day that one takes part in a kidnapping.

And yet... something beyond that wasn't sitting right with Mark at this critical moment. Was it just nerves? Feelings of betrayal for plotting against his friend? It seemed like something more. He couldn't put his finger on it, but his intuition was yelling at him to change course.

The assembled crew began gathering an hour or so later at Aubrey's Burgers, starting with Dr. Kyle Bandon, who was sitting in a booth when Barb and Mark arrived. "Barbara, it's great to see you, circumstances notwithstanding," he said as they approached the table. Kyle was tall and sophisticated-looking with a sharp suit and expensively coiffed golden hair. Mark hated him immediately.

"Good seeing you again, doctor." Barb offered her hand, which Kyle gently shook in a two-handed clasp, wearing a wan smile. The words and actions were professional enough, but Mark sensed that there might be something deeper to this relationship.

The doctor turned to face Mark with an intense stare. "And it's a pleasure to meet you, Mark. This situation probably feels a bit strange, but I assure you that what you're doing is the very best option for your friend."

Mark wasn't buying this. He knew he might be biased against this man due to his slick, imposing stature, but Kyle's words felt both hollow and overly emphasized. Nonetheless, Mark responded with, "thank you." Kyle responded with a lips-pursed nod then waved both of them into the booth. Barb and the doctor made small talk for a few minutes before Mark excused himself.

Once in the bathroom with the door locked, Mark whipped out his phone and called Eve's land line. It rang several times before her answering machine picked up. Mark paused for a moment, trying to figure out what to do, then half-whispered a message, cupping his hand around the bottom of his phone: *"Eve, if you're there, pick up. Actually, I hope you're not there, I... I can't go through with this. Listen to me very carefully — Barb... Barb is coming to have you committed, to a hospital, she's got a, uh... a shrink and a whole crew coming. I... don't know if she's telling the truth about you stalking her or whatever, but... I just, it doesn't... seem... it just... doesn't seem like this should happen. You need to get away from your apartment, right now. I gotta go. Good luck, Eve."* He paused for several more seconds before deciding there was nothing more that needed to be said, then ended the call.

Kyle watched that mousey guy walk away in his peripheral vision, slowly turning his head until he saw Mark turn down the hall leading to the bathroom. His face relaxed and he turned back toward Barb with a slight smile. "Can't help but wonder what the... *real* motive is here," he said quietly, locking eyes with her. Her head titled slightly in bemusement, staring back at him, unfazed. He chuckled. "Hey, not really my business," he added with a wave of his hand.

She faintly smiled back. "Let's just stay focused on the plan, then maybe we can discuss the back story over a drink."

He nodded. "Sure." They both knew that would never happen. So he tried a different route. "How's Bobby?" he asked in an overly friendly, sing-song voice.

This was a trick question: he had literally played golf with the man two days ago. Barb was far too strong to become perturbed by the likes of Kyle Bandon, though he did have some degree of power here, being critical to pulling off the "operation."

"Bobby's... great," she lied, smiling. Fuck off, Kyle.

He chuckled quietly. "Great, that's what I thought."

"And Jeannie?" Two could play at this game.

His eyebrows subtly raised: touché. "Great," he said, still quietly smiling. "Terrific."

He looked down at his watch just as the bell on the diner's front door announced the arrival of another team member.

Eve had cried until there was nothing left. She remained in the same spot on the floor, legs splayed across the living room carpet, torso curled up on the white kitchen linoleum, abdominal muscles tired from quaking, the tequila bottle on its side just behind her head. Half-dried eyes stared lifelessly at the side of a faux wood cabinet. The only sound now was of her short, quiet breaths.

The ring of a telephone scared the bejesus out of Eve, her head lifted reflexively and her breathing jumped to a pant. She regained her awareness and let her head drop again, the air falling out of her chest, slightly wondering who the fuck would be calling right now but also reminding herself that she completely did not give a shit. Still, she was perplexed when she heard the initial machine beep but then nothing immediately after it for a few seconds, and then stunned when Mark's panicked whispers emanated from the speaker. Upon the first mention of "Barb," Eve's head shot up again.

She couldn't believe what she had just heard. Her depressive state competed with Mark's plea until she tossed a few facts over in her mind: Barb was trying to have her committed. She had told him something about stalking. A "crew" was coming. *Now.*

She scrambled to her feet, then froze. They're coming. *They're coming.* Eve turned and looked at the front door, then down at the counter where she had earlier dropped the key. She grabbed it, then stepped toward the door but froze again, realizing she needed... what... something... what? Clothes! She ran to the bedroom, snatched a coat and her gym bag out of her closet, threw in a pair of pants *(they're coming!)*, handfuls of socks, underwear and t-shirts *(a crew, lots of people!)*, jumped into the bathroom for a toothbrush and toothpaste, then bolted back out into the living room. What else? *They're coming!* She was losing time. Was there anything else? She looked into her bag. No, probably not.

Eve jutted toward the front door, reaching into her pocket for the key, then stopped yet again. They might be coming up the hallway *right now.* Even if they were still just walking up the street, they would intercept. If they saw her, they would know that she knew. *They would grab her!* Her eyes widened. She stepped backward, then spun around, breathing rapidly. *The fire escape!*

She ran to the living room window, unlocked and threw it open. She stepped into the opening, one foot on the platform, but stopped again and looked back inside, eyes darting around the room, a last ditch effort to decide if there was anything else to take. She glanced across the stereo cabinet, on which her laptop was sitting. Holy shit, of course she should take that! Eve stepped back into the room, tripping on the window sill and falling onto her gym bag and knocking her head on the corner of the stereo. "FUCK!" She picked herself up and threw the computer and its charger into her bag, then climbed outside and stood on the balcony. After pulling the window down, she froze once more and listened. *Were there voices? Was that a voice?* She couldn't pinpoint it. *Was it behind her, or below?* Eve knew she had no choice but to descend, so she scrambled down the awkward metal ladders, stopping again at the lowest landing to listen and scan before dropping to the alley and bolting into the darkness.

They were an unsettling group, walking across the street together at night: a uniformed cop, two burly nurses in scrubs, and three regularly dressed adults. The officer negotiated entrance to the building with the manager, who led them upstairs to Eve's front door. Quiet as they were attempting to be, the twelve feet made enough commotion to draw open the front doors of three of her neighbors whose reactions ranged from bewilderment to disgust. The manager mainly kept her head down but met the smoldering glare of Eve's neighbor Agnes with a helpless shrug.

The manager rounded the corner of the staircase to Eve's floor, walked past her door, turned around and, with a worried look in her eyes, tilted her head toward the apartment. The cop nodded then turned to Barb and whispered, "You probably should do the honors," before indicating to the rest via hand signals that they should clear away from the periphery of the door's peephole.

Everyone shuffled positions, Mark and the doctor trading places with the nurses. Barb looked back at the group, then took a deep breath and knocked. Nothing — no sound, no response. She tried again. Nothing. She looked over at the officer.

"One more time," he said quietly.

She knocked, adding, "Eve? It's Barb. Please come to the door." She paused again for several seconds before turning again to the officer.

He nodded. "Probably not here, but..." He turned to address the building manager, who solemnly pulled out a ring of keys and walked past him to the door.

The seven-strong crew awkwardly filed into the cramped apartment behind the policeman, who had previously unlatched the leather guard from his gun but seemed noncommittal about it after that point, casually inspecting each of the four small rooms of Eve's home. The only areas even worth giving a second glance were the shower and the closet — otherwise it took all of eight seconds to verify that Eve truly was not present.

A general sense of annoyance and discomfort befell everyone but Mark, who was immensely relieved that his warning was either effective or unneeded. He did his best not to show it, focusing on appearing neutral to the situation. Still, he couldn't hide a sudden, if brief, fixation on the blinking answering machine light, an observation that happened to coincide with Barb's concerned survey of the search party landing on his face. By the time he noticed her, she had noticed the red light.

She made her way around the kitchen counter toward the machine, 'excuse me'-ing past Mark and the two hospital employees who were simply too big for this space. Barb reached the corner of the room and started to make a motion toward the device when...

"DO *NOT* PUSH THAT BUTTON." The officer had his don't-even-think-about-it tone at the ready, having eyed Barb's movements from his position beside the front doorway. Most of the group jumped slightly at the unexpectedly direct voice, then one of the nurses chuckled with a grin on his face. Mark wished he could hug the cop.

Barb paused for a moment, also startled. "But... what if..." she started, pointing at the machine.

"Does not matter," the cop cut her off. "My warrant covers entry and apprehension only. If you touch the patient's property, well..." He looked away into the distance.

Her eyes narrowed, resistant to his insinuation and really wanting a path to hearing the message. "Well... what?"

The officer's face switched to exasperation. "I gotta *arrest* you, that's what!"

The nurses were getting a kick out of this, quietly giggling at Barb's rookie mistake. She recognized her position and lowered her head before walking away from the answering machine and walking back out the doorway, on the way passing a clearly irritated Dr. Bandon, who gave her a pointed stare. Back out in the atrium walkway, Barb stared into space for a few moments while others filed out, then turned around to catch the eyes of Mark, who was caught off-guard after feeling such relief a moment ago.

Internally, Barb remembered her foundation with Mark and put her own anger in check, inhaling and softening her demeanor before looking back up at Mark again with a shrug and a smile. "Mark, you're her buddy. Any ideas?"

After two hours of frantically making her way through a sinuous path out of her neighborhood, using 100% more dark alleyways and momentary hiding places than were necessary (given that there no search party was on her tail), Eve found herself standing in a shadowed space beside a salon, twenty feet from a bus stop. Still scanning her field of view for any danger, *mostly* sure she wasn't seeing movements in trees and bushes nearby, she finally paused to reassess the situation.

What. The. *Fuck.* What the fuck happened here? She leaned against the salon's outer wall and slid down into a crouch. How can this be reality? It is reality, right? Six hours ago... everything was fine. She had been piecing together an outline for a press release about a new contract with the city. During a break she had made small talk in the kitchen with Todd, a junior architect who she wanted to like but couldn't seem to make any real connection with (how utterly irrelevant that was now). Then she was walking back to her desk with a yogurt cup and a spoon when Barb emerged from her office and caught eyes with Eve, who flashed her "office mischief" smile back. Barb remained neutral, asked Eve to come to the office, and then...

Eve took a slow, deep breath and then gasped, realizing she had been daydreaming, quickly glancing side to side again to watch for activity. *Two people emerging from a side street in the distance!* — no, not Barb. She scanned again and found nothing, then squinted into the horizon trying to distinguish bus headlights from the other vehicles lumbering down 10th Avenue. No bus that she could spot— *What is that high-pitched sound?* She held her breath. It stopped. Nothing followed.

Okay, get hold of yourself, reset. Deep breath. Where the fuck was she actually *going* right now? She didn't even know where this bus line led. A terminal, probably, but then what? Hitchhike? Her purse and cell would make all of this so much easier. Shit, she could *fly* away from here if she had those. How could she...

No! Wait a minute, the *backup* door code! Did she even remember what it was? The code wasn't general knowledge, but Barb had told it to Eve over the phone during a logistical snafu months ago. She didn't remember the numbers, but she clearly remembered the shape — it formed a simple 'X' when typed: 1-5-9-3-5-7.

Eve considered the situation for only a few more seconds before realizing that she had to go for it, there was too much to gain by getting there first and collecting her things, and how likely was it that

Barb would go back there? How likely was it that the code had gotten changed already? She bolted.

Mark adopted a thoughtful look, with most of the crew now looking to him for what would happen next. He brought his eyes back to Barb before noticing the attention from the others. "Uh." Long pause. "I... I don't really know. Where... she might go."

Barb pursed her lips and nodded slightly, then quietly sighed, squinting slightly at Mark. Kyle spoke up.

"Look." He shrugged. "If you don't have, I don't know — *strong* evidence of where the girl is, then..." He shook his head. "We're gonna have to depart." Everyone else in the crew was adopting their own pose of impatience: staring at Barb, leaning against the building, watch checking, hallway examining...

She was up against a wall, but not quite ready to give up. Barb turned casually back to Mark. "Okay. So, let's brainstorm. Where have you hung out with Eve in the past?"

Mark's eyebrows went up. "Oh! I... not... many places. I mean, mainly we got lunch together, that sort of thing. We've been to the movies, um..." He looked away at the horizon, feeling confident that this was a dead end, he really didn't know Eve *that* well. They were just work buddies. "We went to a dinner party at my friend's house once."

Different tense reactions from around the group, Barb's exuding the most forced composure. She persisted. "Sure, got it. And, yeah, I guess none of those are exactly... leads." She considered for a moment and got to a different angle. "What... what does Eve *need* right now, in this moment?" She asked the question as much for herself as for Mark.

Kyle tossed an idea in. "Well, she needs shelter at some point — she's abandoned her apartment."

"Good! Yes." Barb nodded approval, measuredly. "But," she bobbed her head side to side, "probably not *right* now, right? I mean, it's not even," checking her watch, "eight o'clock."

"Sure, yeah." Kyle nodded, disengaging again.

Barb turned back over to Mark. "Whatever Eve is doing, wherever she's going... she needs, what. Clothes? Money?"

Mark perked up. "Oh, right. She left..." It was one of those moments where your mouth keeps moving one or two words past the point that your brain has realized you should be shutting up. He paused, stunned at his predicament. But 'she left' was already too much to leave hanging out there. Barb's eyes lasered in on Mark's face.

In a moment of relative confidence, assuming he couldn't be of actual help, Mark had gotten cocky. People who haven't developed a skill in lying don't recognize the importance of remaining in that *mode* — the mode of being careful with every word, every inflection, watching yourself for moves that will give you away — until you're firmly in the clear. Instead, Mark had fallen into his default mode of being a helpful helper. They were brainstorming, right? So when an idea popped into his head, well... out it fell. Enough of it, anyway.

And in the same five seconds the rest of his truth also fell out: that he was not on Barb's side. His suddenly sheepish, surprised reaction at the realization of what he had revealed, as well as the premature end of his statement, made that immediately clear. Barb's suspicion was confirmed. They both knew in that moment that she had him, and that he was going to divulge the rest of that sentence. Barb asked the question calmly and directly. "She left what, Mark?"

Shit. Double shit. What else could he do but answer? "Uh. I..." This kind of pressure was not Mark's strong suit. "I think, she... she might have left..." Quietly, now staring at the floor again. "Her... purse. At the, um... at the office."

Barb's eyes widened. "She what? Her *purse?*" Her eyes darted to Kyle and the others, all of whom were paying more attention now, though not with quite the same renewed fervor as Barb displayed. She looked back over at Mark, whose head was still prone, though his eyes met hers again. "Well then." She turned back to the rest of the crew, now projecting confidence again. "No time to waste, let's get over there." She was able to make a single step in the right direction, but the rest of the group, which was blocking her path, wasn't conforming. Instead, they looked around at one another. "What?" she said, confusedly shaking her head.

Kyle reached up and held the back of his neck. "Barb, I'm sorry, we can't really... *chase* leads here." The cop pursed his lips, turned, and walked away and down the stairs at a leisurely pace. He was only there for a warrant at a specific address, this wasn't otherwise a police operation.

"But..."

"Yeah, look, I get it — it seems obvious to you that she's there, I see the logic," he glanced over at the rest of the guys, who seemed less pissed than a moment ago, but only because they knew this was almost over. "But, A) you can't *know* she's there, and B) there's no reason to think she's there *right now.* You know? How long does it take to secure a purse and get out?"

Barb's eyebrows fell. She knew he was right and now felt stupid again. "Okay, fine. But... what if I go-..." She looked back at Mark. "*We* go over to the office and she's still there?"

"Then call me immediately." Kyle did another quick visual survey. The nurses mildly shrugged — sure, fine. He addressed Barb again. "We'll join you there as soon as we can. If you go now then we won't be far."

"Right, okay." She turned back to her employee, wearing his default look of unease. "Let's move, Mark."

He raised a hand. "Oh, I don't..."

She stopped, turned back to him, then cocked her head with narrowed eyes. "Huh? What's that?" Your move, traitor.

Mark froze. "Yeah, okay."

There wasn't much complicated about this operation other than making sure the coast was clear and verifying (many times) that no abduction crews were on approach. The building had security cameras, and Eve knew she was taking a risk by entering the office, but Eve didn't think it was likely that Barb would be monitoring them. Not yet, anyway.

Still, the few seconds that Eve had to spend under the bright lights of the front door terrified her. Her right hand shook so much that she had to steady it with her left while punching in the code. It was hard to get that X shape wrong, though, and sure enough, the door buzzed her in. She slammed so hard into the metal door handle that it made a crack that she worried would draw attention.

Eve felt so exposed under continued lighting in the lobby that she decided to take the stairs. Four flights later, she panted her way over to the main office door, where she used the same code (this time needing only the one hand) to gain access again. Was this going too well? Was she forgetting something? She didn't see how, but she looked behind her for the fiftieth time before entering.

Eve ran the short distance down the aisle to her desk. Everything was as she had left it, including her yogurt cup, which reminder her of how long it had been since she had eaten. No time to dwell on that now — she threw her phone into her purse and ran out of the office, down the stairs and out of the building.

Once outside, she threw a quick glance up and down the street before pulling her phone back out to call a cab and walking north. Eve waited hidden in the near-dark half a block from her office only a few minutes before flagging down a yellow cab with the light from her phone.

Barb didn't generally wield a lead foot, but this was a rare moment when her BMW served as more than just a status symbol. Mark let out an uncontrollable whimper and gripped whatever he could with both hands as they whipped through the first of several high-speed turns through the twenty or so city blocks to the office, the street lights quietly flying over the car's moonroof as the German motor growled in an aggressive but composed manner. Few cars perused the area at this hour on a weeknight, but twice Barb overtook a vehicle at well above the speed limit. Mark wasn't totally sure he hadn't pissed his pants when they finally arrived at the office block.

Barb's radar was on full alert, and while the taxi rolling past the office building ahead of them didn't raise any interest, she couldn't help but notice, as she squealed to a stop in front of the office door, that the cab's brake lights popped on at a dark spot down the road not in front of any buildings or logical pickup location. Barb froze as she watched a dark figure climb into the cab. A part of her was certain that figure was Eve, another part tugging equally to the hope that she was in the building now.

Mark had started to reach for the door handle after he regained his center but then realized that Barb's manic charge had suddenly halted. He watched her watching the cab but didn't get the inference. "Are... we...?"

Barb raised a single index finger in response, still laser focused on the car now driving away into the night. She took a slow, deep breath, watched the taillights disappear around a corner, paused three more seconds, conflicted, deciding. "Shit" she said, then "let's go" while quickly exiting the car.

The next five minutes were short, intense, and conclusive. Barb and Mark entered and ascended to the fourth floor, keyed into the front door, walked straight to Eve's desk and... no purse evident. Barb was not surprised, and she didn't bother with a desperate "are you sure" or "is this where you saw it?" Eve left her purse on the top of the desk above the file cabinet, that's what she always did. Barb couldn't even look at Mark.

He came up behind her and slowed as he saw that the purse was no longer leaned against the cubicle backdrop where he had seen it last. He took a deep breath and waited a couple of beats, assuming he didn't need to spell the situation out any further, before wondering what should happen next. "Um..."

"Yeah." Barb nodded, her tone was pointed. She also took a deep breath, laser focused on her failure to apprehend the subject, her chin protruding defiantly. Stepping into the cubicle, Barb picked up the tiny ceramic flower pot she had bought for Eve in Portland, Maine last summer, into which Eve had "planted" a hand-crafted flower made of brightly-colored pipe cleaners. She stared at the flower for several seconds before rearing back and hurling it directly at the framed decorative print on the wall beside the cubicle, an ear-splitting crack ensuing as both dissolved into hundreds of shards in every direction.

Mark nearly fell down recoiling from the crash, his eyes wide with shock. Barb stood still, stoically assessing the carnage. A couple more shards dropped out of the poster frame and tinkled onto the floor behind the cubicle.

She calmly turned her steely gaze to Mark, who was frozen in place. With no inflection in tone or change of expression, she asked, "Would you mind cleaning that up?"

Mark tossed a quick glance at the wall before returning it to Barb. His response was only barely perceptible. "N-... no."

Barb walked out of the office without another word.

There are moments in life when some part of your brain realizes you've made a mistake just a hair past the point that you held the ability to change course. Such was the moment that Eve stepped out from the safety of shadow only to glance down the street and spot Barb's gold BMW pull up to a sudden stop in front of the office. A fragment of her mind couldn't decide if it was real, so paranoid had she been up to that point, so ready to spot Barb around the next corner. Eve's heart raced as she continued into the back of the cab, praying that Barb hadn't seen her but knowing that she almost certainly had.

"DRIVE, NOW. PLEASE." The cabbie complied, then Eve turned around to watch. She could see two silhouettes and assumed one was Mark. No movement, which meant Barb was watching. Considering.

This was a long, straight street, and suddenly Eve realized that she needed first and foremost to get out of Barb's line of sight. "Take your first turn, please."

"Which-..."

"Doesn't matter, just turn." She continued to watch their trail, the previous road falling into the distance, no golden sedan materializing.

No time to relax, though. "Take your next left." He did. "Uh... go two blocks and turn right. *No, three blocks.* One more block. Sorry." They followed a rabbit's trail roughly northeast through a residential section of the city, Eve's gaze glued to the back window. After ten minutes, it was clear that they were safe.

She faced forward. A long silence followed as Eve's awareness reset. Now what?

"So..." the cab driver began. He was coming to a T intersection.

"Oh! Sorry. Um..." Eve wasn't entirely certain about her next move. "Can... you pull over for a second?" The driver complied. "And turn off the headlights?" He did, and was aware enough of the situation to also put the car in park and remove his foot from the brake, then hit a dashboard switch that also turned off the backseat cab TV facing her. She took a deep breath. The houses and condos on this block were really dark. Eve's mind raced through potential destinations. All of them felt shut down by Barb's actions.

Well then. "The airport, please."

She was safe. For now. Probably. Eve slid down in her seat, head against the seat back, trying to get her mind right, the cab TV's inane ads a blur. Barb. Mark. A crew. It's over. Her job. Her life in this city. Her soulmate. Her future. Everything... gone. She felt a familiar mixture of sorrow and emptiness, nothing to latch onto, no emotional hooks to pull her towards crying or raging.

Her gaze fell downward to where her hand was resting in her lap. She realized she was still wearing the expensive sapphire/silver ring that Barb had bought for some anniversary last year. She pulled the ring off and looked at it for a few seconds before dropping it to the floor, her gaze still on the naked finger. Her eyes then wandered upward to the TV, where they widened. Her heart raced. Oh. My. God.

Eve's mouth slowly turned into a smile as she turned to look up into the sky, bridge lights passing overhead as they turned onto the interstate. She chuckled quietly, then fell into convulsive laughter. It was just too good.

"Just the drink, thanks." The waiter returned her smile, nodded and marched over to the bar. Eve took a deep breath and settled back into her cushy booth at whatever cheesy, over-priced airport bar-restaurant this was. A plane ticket to Boston lay on the table beside her. She closed her eyes, elated. It was bizarre to be so *happy* about what she had decided, she had to keep reminding herself how dark it actually was. But she just... couldn't be sad about it. It was perfect. It was so perfect.

She HATED that chair. Ever since Barb brought that suicide chair to Eve's attention, blathering about how "brilliantly dark" it was, how "honest" and "visceral" — it made Eve want to puke once she realized what the chair was for, it struck her, like a gut punch, with essentially the opposite reaction: she thought it was a shitty, disgusting, inhumane excuse for "art." Eve seldom understood Barb's explanations about the art world, but mostly she just nodded and secretly disdained the painting created with bodily fluids, the garden watering can cut in half on its side, the middle-aged white woman wearing only a nun's habit sitting in a barber's chair for five hours asking "now?" every five seconds. But no, not that fucking chair. She couldn't keep quiet about that one. Something about it just... infuriated her. That was one of their loudest fights. Things were broken. Barb stormed out.

So yeah, when some news story about that chair popped up on the taxi TV... oh, the *timing* of it! It was kismet. It was a sign. If ever there was a way to be done, just *done* with all of this AND screw Barb over, by way of a detailed note that would simply have too many important details for Barb to pass it off as Eve's imagination, this was it. Ending it all on the world stage, in the famous chair. She smiled again.

That thought led back to Barb's actions today. Yeah, okay, maybe Eve had crossed a line going to Barb's house unannounced. Eve didn't want to think much more about that, didn't want to wonder how that had factored into Barb suddenly cutting things off. But *committal?* Turning everyone against her, shutting Eve's life down entirely? What the fuck was that? Fuck that. Fuck her. *Fuck everything.*

The waiter startled Eve back to reality with her drink order: top shelf tequila on ice with a splash of triple sec. Eve stared down at it, the anticipation of its cold, sharp liquid shifting her mood away from anger and toward the satisfaction of impending revenge. She picked it up, slowly brought it to her lips and drank half of it down. Heaven.

Still holding the drink, she glanced over at the TV above the bar. Ha! The chair was there again! Eve laughed and started to gesture a toast to the chair when something else appeared on the screen — an ambulance. Then a body bag. A photo of a young boy. A headline: "Death By Famous Suicide Chair."

No.

No.

NO.

The glass fell from Eve's hand onto the table, where it bounced loudly then fell onto its side, the contents spilling over the edge of the table to the wood floor, drawing wary attention from a handful of patrons and staff.

Eve was frozen. She couldn't breathe.

Blank minutes passed. When she regained awareness, the waiter asking for the sixth or seventh time if she was okay, she had trouble remembering what was happening. The glass was upright again on a coaster, the table wiped dry. Finally, she looked up at him. "What?"

"Are you-..."

"Yes." She understood only enough to crystallize what he had been asking and give out a default response. "I'm... fine."

He squinted his eyes for a moment, considering both whether he should believe her and whether he should follow his default script of offering another drink. "Okay. Then, um..." He flipped a couple of pages over on his pad and ripped one off. "Here's the bill, take your time."

Her eyes followed the paper to the table and stayed there. The waiter paused for half a second more then walked uneasily away.

Airport. The chair. Barb. She glanced at the boarding pass. Boston. Why go there now? What reason is there to move from this spot, why not just let this last breath out and die here in this vinyl booth?

The tinny, electronic blare of Missy Elliott broke that train of thought — her cell phone ringing from the purse beside her. She pulled it out and looked at the caller ID: Mark.

She pondered. Mark. Mark sold her out. But... then he tipped her off. Was he still on her side? Did she even give a shit?

She sighed. Fuck it.

She flipped the phone open and paused for a moment before quietly saying, "Hi, Mark."

"Oh my god, Eve — you answered, I'm so glad!" She wasn't sure she had ever heard him this animated. "Listen, Eve, I don't know where you went, but — I mean, it doesn't matter, don't tell me — look, I am *so sorry* about tonight, I can't believe I... just... bailed on our friendship, that I took Barb's side over yours, she... I don't know, she told me things that... look, sorry, it doesn't matter."

He took a breath and a pause. "Eve. I'm on your side now, I swear. That shit that Barb pulled, not just on you, but on ME, goddammit... the more I thought about it, the angrier I got! That fucking... *cunt-*" You could tell that once a once-per-decade word for Mark, "bullied me like I was in middle school! I'm a GROWN FUCKING MA-... sorry, sorry, I'm still... really jacked up... hey, you're still there, right?"

"Uh, yeah." If nothing else, this was a change of pace for Eve's state. All she could do was receive all of this charged energy coming out of her phone's speaker.

"Good, okay, look. I don't care what it takes, I don't care about my fucking job at this point. I don't even fucking care if you actually stalked Barb or whatever." He paused. "I want to make amends for helping her almost ruin your life. I want revenge. For both of us."

He stopped, clearly giving Eve space to try the proposal on. Eve could *barely* process this moment, yet another precipice in half a day of terrifying cliff edges. She glanced around at the bar/airport scene around her, then back at her ticket. It felt like a strange past all of a sudden. Her gut told her the only way was forward.

Eve took a deep breath.

"Okay."

"Not my problem, piss-ant." Lee Adkins' hands hurt. So did the muscles in his back and shoulders, but his hands were so badly marred that people usually assumed he suffered from a skin disease. He just had to deal with the pain and hope that nothing in the filthy dishwater would make those assumptions correct. The restaurant manager couldn't care less — Lee would clean up the piles of dishes that Drew had abandoned or he would look for another job, and Lee was in no position to do that. Bussing and washing dishes was just about all he was qualified to do, and the scar running across left jaw and down his neck disqualified him even for that in some restaurants.

The scar was a daily reminder of his sometimes senile, often incarcerated, now dead uncle Troy, who had slashed at Lee with a kitchen knife in a fit of rage when Lee was just six years old, banging on a toy drum that Troy's girlfriend had given him for Christmas. Questionable as her choices in men were, she was one of the few people who had ever been kind to Lee, which only seemed to fuel Troy's anger. Troy had taken her life before making the decision to give up his own in a phenomenally misguided battle with the local police over a decade ago.

Lee's mother was expecting him to be home before his brother's recital so that he could keep an eye on the dog, who had been inexplicably leaving messes around the apartment. Lee would probably get a thrashing for not showing up, but less than the one he would get if he came home unemployed.

"Take Danny to the music building," Lee's mother said from her plastic-covered lounge chair without looking at him, watching Family Feud with a cigarette in her hand. "He'll be done in an hour, just stay and wait. Get milk on the way home."

Lee stood still for several seconds looking in vain for some way of objecting, but knew that would be pointless. She was aware that he planned to go out for the evening and didn't care. Lee was the product of a marriage that had failed so miserably that his mother wanted to erase from her past everything related to it. Daniel was the product of another failed marriage, but because he had inherited a gift for music (his father's only redeeming trait) he was the primary focus of her life, and the best role Lee could ever aspire to was as an aid in Daniel's success. Daniel had originally taken a noncommittal attitude to this arrangement, but through the constant encouragement directed at him and the constant abuse directed at Lee, Daniel had gradually inherited a similar disdain for his less favored older brother. Daniel knew he could jab Lee at will without fear of recourse. No one cared.

All the other characters in Lee's home life were bit-parts played by his mother's routinely rotating boyfriends, most of whom fit the ignorant, belligerent, white-trash drunk mold. And since they would face her most vehement wrath (read: gunpoint) if ever they laid a hand on the cherished Daniel, Lee became their de facto punching bag.

Since Lee's mother was nearly always in front of the television, Lee seldom got a chance to watch it, but he had twice now overheard something on the news about a suicide chair, and this morning he had gotten a closer look at what all the commotion was about — it was on the covers of two of the news magazines at the stand beside the restaurant. It was apparently supposed to be a piece of art, though Lee didn't really understand what would make it so.

+

It wasn't that Dom hadn't noticed girls before Karen. He had even made-out with a few, mostly the smitten ones who stalked the "broody artist" at a skating rink or a party. Nor was he a virgin, thanks to an experience that was so irrevocably awkward that he and the only official girlfriend he had by that point both questioned their very existence afterward (and then agreed, by way of completely avoiding one another, that the relationship was over). It wasn't that Dom hadn't noticed girls, but something about Karen caught him by surprise, ever so subtly jolted his system. It was in a Drawing 102 class that he laid and then kept eyes on her.

The class in question was Northeastern University in Boston, 200 miles South of Cape Johns. Despite remaining a bit on the baby-faced side, Dom was tall and "artsy" enough that he could pass for a college undergrad even though he was only 16 and taking college art classes well ahead of schedule. Karen was on a more typical scholastic track, and therefore two years his senior. Focused and intensely shy, it took her quite awhile to realize that Dom was staring at her as much as he was studying the nude model almost directly in between them.

Twenty minutes into their session, she shifted her glance just briefly as she realized the dark-haired boy across the room was looking at her. Immediately her eyes locked onto her paper, and for a moment Dom worried that he had made her uncomfortable. But when he subtly stole one more glance in her direction, he caught a controlled grin on her face. That was all the reassurance he needed, and he concentrated mainly on his work for the duration of the class.

She was too quick for him when the class ended — the professor pulled him aside (they almost always did, feeling a need either to "mentor" him or in some other way make an impression on the Boy Who One Day May Be King) long enough that he could no longer track her down when he finally walked out of the studio. But he lucked out in the Humanities courtyard late that afternoon, where he spotted her nose-deep in a textbook, yellow notepad at her side, sitting with her back to a maple tree. The area was only lightly populated with other students who were alternately studying, conversing or kicking a hacky sack around. It had been on the chilly side for much of the day, but by that point the air had struck a temperature so perfect as to feel electric. Dom felt inspired.

He deliberately walked around to her side, giving her a wide berth so as to avoid her spotting him, then casually made his way into her field of vision roughly twenty feet away, where he sat on a low boulder, facing her direction but knowing that she was too fixated on her studies to notice him immediately. He then pulled a small sketchbook and a pencil out of his bag and commenced to drawing her from afar.

As before, it took several minutes for her to discover what was happening, and Dom had to exaggerate his artist-in-portrait-mode performance a bit with the traditional "squinting with tongue out and using the thumb as a guide" gesture in order to finally get her attention. She did a little double-take before recognizing him and stifling a grin while looking down and flushing red. She tried, or at least pretended, to return to her studies but couldn't help looking back at Dom while he found more ways to demonstrate how seriously he was taking this venture: shaking his head, holding the sketchbook up to compare rendition to reality, tapping his lips with his finger before erasing, holding his finger up with an "ah-HA!" look, then furiously drawing again...

After five minutes of this routine, Dom stood, nodded satisfactorily at the page with cocked eyebrow, tore it from his sketchbook and folded it over, then threw his bag over his shoulder and walked toward Karen, who looked up at him sheepishly. He slowed as he approached her but didn't stop, instead holding the folded page out to her with two fingers as he casually walked past, slyly grinning as she took it from him. Without a word or a look back, he continued walking away. Karen watched him do so, a bit surprised, then turned back and opened the page. It contained a simple, carefully drawn smiley face. Below that was his phone number and the words, "See you in class, cutie."

"Damnedest thing," rookie officer Olnik said with a grin, walking backward toward the shop and shaking his head dramatically. "Still daylight, right, the kid smashes the front window of this place." He gestures inside. "Totally bypasses the guitars, all those fancy electronic gadgets on that rack there — doesn't steal a thing, right? Walks past all of it." Olnik held up an index finger, grinning giddily, then stepped around the splatter of broken glass outside the shop and through its doorway. He was getting a kick out of what appeared to be a bizarre but straightforward case (most cases were neither). No doubt he would regale this story to his girlfriend tonight, and to anyone else who would listen for the rest of his life. "What does he do instead? *That.*"

He pointed to a train wreck of what was, until recently, a glossy baby grand piano. The body was tilted forward to the floor thanks to a busted front leg. A smattering of keys were strewn about, leaving previously hidden plungers behind. Broken strings hung out the side of the smashed-in top cover. It resembled the carcass of a defeated wild animal.

Detective Garner looked over the wreckage then back to the lieutenant with no change of expression. "And you know it was a kid how?"

"Oh, dude—" he caught himself. "Uh, sorry—*sir.* That's the best part! Look!" He pointed up at the very large, obvious video camera that might have been cutting edge twenty years prior. It was less than twenty feet from the piano and featured a blinking red light that should have gotten the attention of anyone looking to destroy a $20,000 instrument. "We've already looked at the footage, it's clear as crystal! We sent it over to Records, they're checking it against juvie mugs now."

He was still grinning expectantly, but the detective was less amused by the scene. He had been thick in the compiling of evidence on a decidedly *difficult* case when he got pulled down here for this complete waste of his time. "I believe you and your partner have control of this situation, am I right?"

Olnik's grin dropped. "Oh, uh. Yes, yes sir, no prob—"

"Great," Garner responded, turning to leave. "Let me know if you see anything unusual."

Lee had fucked up royally. Petty theft would have been one thing, but that was some expensive hardware that he had decimated. He couldn't quite figure out why he had done it — it wasn't even Daniel's piano — and he wouldn't be sure that he had done it at all if he hadn't heard the sirens coming, held up the metal pipe in his bloodied hands, then looked down at the broken wreck. All he knew now, panting desperately as his flight away from the music shop slowed, was that hell he had never known would be waiting for him at home. The whole family would be participating this time for sure. Flashes of belts, bats, bottles, and fists ran through Lee's mind has he stopped and collapsed onto the cold, wet sidewalk.

Lee was scared, probably more so than the day he got his scar. He had nearly lost his balance a couple of times as he ran, so dominating and distracting were the images in his mind. The only sound Lee could hear beyond the pounding of his own heart was the thumping of his boots against the concrete. It was only eight blocks from here to his building. He wished it was as many miles.

The fear built up in his throat as he rounded the last corner, praying he wouldn't see any activity at his building. Luck was not on his side — a police cruiser was parked in front, two cops standing at his door. He nearly jumped out of his skin backward, falling onto the ground and yanking his exposed foot back around the corner. He breathed furiously in terror for a few seconds before leaping up and sprinting in the opposite direction.

What the fuck was he thinking? Why would he go home anyway, knowing the police would probably catch up to him there eventually? He ran without thinking for a few minutes, back down the street, as fast as his legs and lungs would carry him, but was forced to stop and rest not far from the restaurant that no longer employed him. He leaned against the nearest wall, panting, but suddenly he felt very vulnerable and jumped into a nearby alleyway, where he slumped against a garbage bin.

Lee considered his situation, trying to come up with a plan for running away, but the limited options at his disposal vanished immediately when he realized that the cops would almost certainly catch him anywhere — that scar was hard for anyone to miss. And then... back here again, back to all-consuming torment. Fear. Hatred. The belt, the cane, the bottle.

They came at him all at once, a litany of competing emotions. Fear and hatred of his mother, his brother, and just about everyone else he had ever known. Frustration with his dead-end life. Despair over a future of — assuming he lived through the punishment that awaited him — waiting hand and foot on Daniel while receiving unrelenting verbal and physical abuse from everyone involved, or just leaving and living on the street, never to break into a comfortable existence. An all-too-familiar pain of helpless torment poured down his spine, and Lee realized he was moaning through a fountain of tears. For several minutes he cried into his hands.

Finally, he settled somewhat. A breathy whimper left his mouth as he leaned his head back against the bin and wiped tears out of his reddened eyes, which he then opened and allowed to focus. Then he fell silent, breathless. On the wall across from him in the alley was a bold, brightly-colored poster, ten feet tall, containing an image that had recently become familiar, an image that at this moment finally took on a meaning that had been lingering in the back of his mind for weeks, waiting for the right elements to align in his consciousness. The chair.

It was a poster for that chair. The chair that everyone was talking about. The chair that was in an art gallery just a few miles from here.

It's funny how a person who has been ignored his entire life can develop a sixth sense for how to do so intentionally. Making it past the admission desk without being noticed was no amazing feat, but finding a safe hiding place just two rooms away from the most famous sculpture in the country was a task that only a neglected shrew like Lee would be capable of. Breaking into a facility like this at night was beyond his abilities, but he knew that remaining inside when the security systems went online was mostly a matter of being savvy. The shelter he chose was a utility closet just inside the doorway to the men's bathroom, and no one batted an eye when he opened it, stepped inside and closed the door.

An hour or so later the lights dimmed. Lee waited patiently until the shuffling of the cleaning crew died down (once someone even came inside to deposit a mop bucket, but there was plenty of room behind the door for Lee to remain concealed), then stood still for another half hour to make sure there was no other noise. He gently turned the latch of the door and pushed it a couple of inches outward, carefully scanning his available field of vision for bodies. He knew better than to make assumptions, and took great care to move slowly and check his surroundings quickly. No one was in the first room, nor the next, though Lee wouldn't have noticed if there were, so awestruck was he by what lay before him.

The raw magnificence of the chair frightened him to the core. The black frame stood rigid in the air like a warrior at attention, arms hanging down in a stance of readiness. The coiled spring and conical spike gleamed like the chrome armaments he had seen in medieval war movies. If he hadn't already seen it in photographs, Lee probably would have turned and run for his life. The bulk of the piece might have been mistaken for a shadow, so muted were its surfaces. The gleaming steel implements at its base seemed so potent and deadly that Lee was compelled to step lightly for fear of setting them off.

He was mesmerized. Lee had simply never been confronted by such a magnificent thing, and certainly had never been in the presence of any significant work of art. For several minutes he did nothing but trace a slow, wide circle around the chair, marveling at the perfection of its angles and surfaces.

Finally he came full circle to face the chair and stepped forward, over the black felt guard rope. He reached down and lightly grazed the smooth anodized surface of the seat, admiring its perfection. He paused, trying to brush away his confusion and remember what he was doing there. He stood upright and looked away from the chair and to the empty doorways on either side of the room, gathering his wits. He thought of his mother and brother, and his eyes again fell to the chair. Fine art like this was almost certainly in his brother's future; someday soon Daniel would probably make it rich, and when that happened, his mother would see to it that Lee would never again share his family's walls. That was why he was here. For the first time in his life, Lee was in control of his own destiny. He was here to go down on his own terms, and to throw a giant, bloody wrench into his mother's plans.

Lee stared at the hole in the chair's back. The bottom edge caught the dim moonlight like an amber moon crescent. He leaned forward enough to see through the hole the spike's imperceptibly sharp tip protruding through a gleaming ring that held the spring in place. He wanted very much to fold the chair back with his hands and see the bolt snap, to get a demonstration of this instrument of death before giving himself to it, but he knew that would be the end of his plan. Lee understood very little about machines, but he could see that the bolt was not meant to snap back into place once it had fired. There was just one thing left to do.

He took a deep breath and turned to face the opposing wall. Through a row of windows just below the ceiling, he saw a net of stars piercing the clear night sky. Slowly he bent his shaking legs. It was an effort to force them to do so, as though gravity was coaxing him back into the air. His butt made contact with the rigid seat and he shuddered.

The chair was high enough that he could only just sit in it with his toes still touching the floor. Again he looked up at the night sky, then eased backward against the trunk of the chair. Its heavy bulk required a bit of force but slid smoothly on its hinge once it was set in motion. Although he had noticed during his earlier inspection the leg board hanging from the end of the seat, it was still startling to feel it push his legs forward. It had not dawned on him that the chair was designed to leave its occupant laying straight as a board.

The mechanism was apparently designed to move gracefully no matter what; it resisted falling backward with gravity and required a steady push to maintain the reclining motion. Its movement was wholly remarkable in its smoothness — the minute hiss of the flexing hinges was the only perceptible sound besides the faint rustling of Lee's clothes. He was ignoring the hanging armrests, his sweaty hands firmly gripping the sides of the seat. The further back he leaned, the more rapid his breathing became. He got about halfway down before he panicked and quickly leaned forward, dropping his legs to either side of the leg board even though it was already falling slowly downward, as the chair's back raised to its upright position. He looked down at his shaking hands and heaving chest, trying to regain his calm. Sweat ran down his forehead.

Lee had not been raised in a religious environment. His mother was about as godless as they come, and Lee had never known his supposedly Christian father. Still, he felt this must be as good a time as any to make the last of a handful of prayers he had recited during his lifetime. "G-God..." he said before awkwardly bringing his hands together, alternately trying them pressed and clasped before settling on something in between. "I'm... I'm sorry for... what I'm doing, here. I... I just want them... it all... to stop, for the hurting to stop. And to be... something. For people... to see me as somebody other than a, um... like, a dish washer or something. I hope... I, um... please have... please have mercy on me... on my soul." His hands separated briefly before he brought them together for a final, "Amen."

The prayer had taken his mind off of the task long enough to set him more at ease. He stared into the wall for a moment, then scooted back against the chair. Again he pressed and fell backward, but this time he allowed his arms to lay against the armrests. He could hear nothing this time, so loud was the pulsing of blood in his ears. The slow transition to the laying position was so smooth that he almost forgot what lay at the end. His tension grew as he straightened out — it seemed to be taking forever to reach the bottom. Perhaps he was unwittingly putting less pressure on the chair as he went down, prolonging the inevitable.

He thought for the briefest of moments that he could feel a delicate click just before the silence was split like lightning by an ear-splitting, metallic crack, and a searing combination of pains was quickly replaced by utter torment. All that was Lee Adkins struggled silently against the intruding object, every muscle clenched in a vain effort to rise up and away from the bloody weapon that now extended several inches out of his shattered sternum, and that had forced his previously flat back into a constricted arc. For several seconds he thinly gasped into the silence while the portion of his mind that wasn't devoted to surviving attempted to make sense of the metal object sticking into the air. His eyes were bulging nearly out of their sockets, rapidly turning blood red. His arms, wire-taught with tendons rippling, reached inward against their own tension to grasp the object but were frozen several inches out. Tears ran down his temples, and blood from his nose.

The struggle ended abruptly as his oxygen-deprived nervous system issued its last command. His unconscious head fell to the metal surface with a deep, quiet thud. The final remnant of air escaped his lungs in a gurgle as his arms dropped, one onto a rigid armrest and the other in between the second rest and the chair's trunk.

Dom sighed and looked up at Ferron Tower with a longing to climb up and start sketching. The sun would be peeking over the water's edge soon, just the right time to catch the interlaced patterns of the industrial piping across the bay. For all his fame and sudden success, he sorely missed those morning sessions. Spare time was a luxury not appearing in his foreseeable future. Even now he was in a rush to make an 8 AM flight.

He pulled up to the gallery's security gate in his new Saab just as the morning guard was sitting down with a fresh cup of coffee. "Morning, Leo!"

"Hey, mornin,' Mr. Winters," Leo answered while hitting the gate switch. "You here to polish that deathtrap of yours?"

Dom smiled. "Sure am."

Leo shook his head and said, "I can't believe you got time to polish that thing yourself, Mr. Winters."

"Ah, gotta *make* time for it, Leo. I wouldn't be able to live with myself if somebody hurt themselves on it."

Leo grinned. "Hey, you don't have to tell me twice — I ain't going nowhere near that damned thing."

Dom laughed, waved and pulled into the garage. He parked in a staff space since he knew he would be finished and gone before most of the employees arrived anyway. He waved his security card past the scanner and entered the building, which, from the looks of it, was still empty.

Dom grabbed a couple of cloth diapers and a can of Pledge from his locker and walked toward the west wing, going over the day's schedule in his head: touch down in Chicago at 9:40 and take a cab to the PBS affiliate (need to find out what the call letters are), brunch with AIC dean Edgar Davis before a noon flight to Dallas, check into the Hilton and wait for the Art Forum interviewer to call, maybe get in a nap before the evening gala next door...

That last phrase reverberated in his head as he swung through *The Conclusion's* doorway. He could hear the words "gala next door" repeating, but couldn't make himself remember what they meant because of the competing image that lay before him. "Gala," he muttered to himself one last time before his mind put away the gala question and switched instead to confusion over what wasn't right about the picture he saw. Like a person's life flashing before their eyes in their last moments, Dom's mind ran, during the next several seconds, through every conceivable option other than the truth. A joke? A hallucination? Some sort of ambitious graffiti? A similar, new addition to the museum? All ridiculous answers to any but the desperately hopeful or profoundly stunned, and Dom was both.

When reality set in, so did the shock. The heart beat furiously while the lungs did nothing. He didn't feel his knees hit the floor as he collapsed with his eyes transfixed on the blood-covered spike and the pale face of the victim, frozen in terror. The Pledge can fell with a clang to the wooden floorboards. A part of Dom's mind that was still unwilling to admit to the situation contemplated his previously untested sculpture's design flaws: there should have been holsters around the armrests and blinders to either side of the leg board, perhaps a thin gutter outlining the trunk section, to catch the dark red mess that now stained the metal coil and formed a puddle in the floor beneath. Though Dom instinctively tried to yell for help, all that surfaced was a breathless hiss. His mind continued to fight against the image, trying despondently to erase the truth, when finally it got its wish as he passed out and toppled sideways into a fetal position.

Blissful was the briefly ignorant period when he came to, wondering only for a moment why he was laying on a wooden floor with a pair of diapers in front of him, then praying that the coarse, broken image in his mind had been a bad dream. But the reality of the situation would not be suppressed. Dom couldn't bring himself to look at the body again. With fear and sadness running through his soul he turned away and placed his hands on the floor in front of him, shakily lifting himself to his feet. With great effort he placed one foot in front of the other and walked out of the room.

Alex drove up to the cordoned-off museum an hour later. Susan Brown, a curator he had dealt with when evaluating gallery spaces for the chair, had called to fill him in after realizing that Dom wasn't going to. He waved her down from outside the police tape and she motioned to the officers to let him in. She was finishing a cigarette outside the museum entrance, and for a few seconds they just stared at each other in silence.

Susan dropped and snuffed out her stub. She stared at the ground and said, "He's quiet, but I think he's okay. I guess."

Alex nodded and walked inside. There were only a few cops and museum staff members here, but in the distance he could see the fringe of the activity near the entrance to the west wing. No doubt the body had long since been removed, but the documentation and processing still had a ways to go. He had no desire to see what was left of the crime scene. Dom sat in a folding chair near a wall at the opposite end of the hallway, staring into space.

Alex walked up and stood beside him. He reached out and placed his hand on Dom's shoulder but said nothing. The two of them remained there for a few minutes in silence while dim voices and camera snaps emanated from the next room, then Alex walked over to what appeared to be the officer in charge and said, "Excuse me, Officer, um..."

"Thompson."

"Officer Thompson," he said and smiled meekly. "Do you know when Mr. Winters will be allowed to leave?"

"He's allowed to leave now — I told him so a little while ago." He was trying to be polite but was mostly focused on the report he was filling out. "Just needs to stay in town, in case we have any further questions."

"Okay. Thank you," Alex said and turned to Dom again. He walked over and knelt down beside him. "Dom." Dom didn't move. "We should leave, Dom. Let's go home. Come on." He stood and pulled gently on Dom's arm. Dom hesitated for a moment and then rose. Alex spotted a news van past the front entrance and opted for a side door.

He decided that Karen's home would be better right now than Dom's. After parking, Alex walked around the car and opened Dom's door. "Come on, buddy."

Dom turned his head to the right, looked up and realized where he was. "Why are we here?"

Alex thought it over for a second. "I just think you'll be better off at Karen's place right now, Dom. You shouldn't be alone right now."

Karen had seen them from the window and was waiting with the door open. "Hey, sweetie," she said quietly while coaxing Dom toward the couch.

Alex pulled her aside before she sat down. "I really need to go back to the museum and see what's going to happen next."

"Sure. It's fine, I'll take care of him. Come back when you can, though, okay?" Alex nodded and walked out, back toward his car. It had started to rain. Karen considered the delicate streaks of water on the dusty glass of her storm door, then turned to Dom, who sat like a pile of old clothes on the couch. What could she say? This didn't feel like a moment when verbal reassurance would be of any help. Instead, she walked over and sat down beside him, draped her arm across his shoulders, gently placed her other hand on his belly, laid her head on his shoulder, and took a slow breath.

Dom sat motionless, staring off into the distance...

How old was I, five? Six? I can still feel the sun cooking my arms, the tacky rubber on that giant, faded basketball. The dry, barren earth that was our court. The green of the woods around us, the wispy blue sky, the songs of birds, the sporadic rattles of leaves. And my mom. In a green sweatshirt and jeans, telling me to try again. There was no such thing as pressure, it was just a little game to be played. The moment couldn't have been more innocent. I squinted my eyes in the sunlight, looking up at the basket, miles away. Even getting it up there wasn't a given, but she told me I could do it, so I believed her. Held the ball to my shoulder, crouched to one side and hurled it at the sky with everything I had. It hit the backboard, bounced twice on the rim and dropped through the hoop. Her reaction enveloped me, cheering me on and lifting me up into her arms. My heart soared. I was high as a kite.

No paint. No pencils. And I couldn't convey that feeling with a canvas anyway.

The memory faded. Dom looked to his side and saw Karen staring back at him. The ghost-white face of a dead teenager flashed in his mind, eyes fixed in a stunned stare, dried blood streaming from his blackened mouth down his cheek. Dom lurched forward and emptied his stomach onto the coffee table, ruining a loose stack of magazines before Karen emptied a decorative bowl of its pinecones and put in front of him. He kept heaving long after there was nothing left to release, his body trying in vain to eject the horror it now contained. Karen remained at his side, brushing tousled hair from his sweating brow, stroking his back. If there was a polar opposite to that sunny, innocent moment of childhood victory, this was it.

An unnerving silence hung in the air. The chaos surrounding the "incident" had subsided — paramedics and their vehicles had left with the body, forensics experts had vacated the site with their photos and samples, and only two tired police officers remained to guard the crime scene. Alex leaned against the wall opposite *The Conclusion's* bloody, cordoned-off display space, his head hanging forward, eyes fixed to the floor. He was pale, tired, emotionally drained. "He never dreamed that anyone would use it, I'm sure of that." His voice was delicate and slow. "Kinda naive, I guess, but Jesus... how... how could it have happened so *quickly?*"

Susan sat in a chair beside the corridor, staring at the white sky outside the narrow windows near the ceiling of the gallery, looking just as spent. She sighed. They had all known (probably more than Dom, who was utterly enamored with his creation) that it was a risk; the piece wouldn't have been such a success if it wasn't so dangerous. "No point in wondering about it all now, really. What's done is done. I'm sure the press will analyze the hell out of it, tell us all the myriad reasons why the kid did it." She ignored the moving shadows in her peripheral vision: those same reporters, locked out of the building, waiting for a quote from anyone involved. "Alex, I think you should probably head home, try to get some rest. Let's use the back door."

A few of the lingering reporters were smarter than that — they gambled on the back door and caught Susan escorting Alex to his car.

Alex saw them coming and veered Susan in the opposite direction. The reporters wouldn't be thwarted, and began barking questions...

"Could you comment on the suicide-... Did Dom know the victim-... How did he get into the museum-... Could this have been an accident-... How does Dom feel about-... Is this what Mr. Winters had planned all along?"

That last one flipped a switch inside of Alex. He stopped cold, eyes wide, and dove sideways at the question's source before either man had any idea what was happening. With two handfuls of jacket and dress shirt, Alex shoved the reporter to the concrete and locked eyes with a mix of fury and fear. Susan immediately dropped to the ground and pulled at Alex's arm.

"No, Alex! This won't help him. *Please.*"

Alex's face softened slightly, still staring deeply into his victim's eyes. He took a breath and calmly said, "No," before standing up, straightening his jacket and walking away.

If there's one benefit that veteran cops don't get, it's being spared the terrible duty of reporting deaths to loved ones. Rookies just can't be counted on to hold the proper level of decorum, or to emotionally stomach the stunned heartache that appears on the faces of those who have just lost someone they've held dear for most or all of their lives.

And Jesus Christ, what do you tell the mother of a boy who just eviscerated himself on a world-famous sculpture? Sergeant Frank Eldred hated this part of his job, it broke his heart every time he was called upon to perform it, and he was thankful that his script was mostly written for him by city regulations. Lord knows he wouldn't know how to deliver this news on his own.

And had he ever delivered such news in a ritzy neighborhood? Not once. Bay Park was the typical shithole that poor dregs like Lee Adkins nearly always came from. Eldred cast a wary eye over the jimmy-rigged staircase leading up to Adkins' former residence, then climbed up to the second floor of the low-income rental building. He found apartment #34, took a deep breath and knocked.

Behind the screen door appeared an aging, barefoot, stub-smoking woman in a tattered plaid shirt and denim shorts. She stood in the doorway and peered cynically at the officer.

Sgt. Eldred said, "Good afternoon, ma'am. Are you the mother of..."

"Goddammit, what the *fuck* did that shithead do now?!" she started yelling before Sgt. Eldred could even finish his sentence. "God fucking *dammit*, I am sick and tired..."

Eldred broke in, holding up his hand. "Mrs. Adkins, please, it's not like that." His voice slowed and softened. "I'm very sorry to inform you... that your son Lee was found dead inside the Fizi Art Museum this morning."

There was never any way to predict what came next. Parents lost their breath, cried, screamed, fell to the floor, became delirious, or furious... any combination of the above. A couple of them had passed out. One had simply started crying without moving a single facial muscle, then walked away.

But this... this was a new one. The strangest reaction Sgt. Eldred had ever gotten. This woman stared with thoughtful eyes at him for a good ten seconds, motionless, then her gaze softened, she looked into the distance over Eldred's shoulder, and a slight but unmistakable *smile* appeared on her face as she closed the door on him without saying another word. Eldred stood confused for a several moments, unsure of how to proceed, then slowly walked away.

✛

Watership Elementary was more or less as Dom had remembered it, albeit with a couple of cheap annex buildings now attached and some new paint colors here and there. Faculty faces and bodies were a dozen years older/wider as well. And the hallways had shrunk. That was the most surreal part.

Dom had spent two years in Watership's art program between ages four and five. The Winters family was lucky that they had local access to a public school with a strong commitment to the arts, and Dom's mother had negotiated a special arrangement with the school's visual art teacher, Evelyn Kennedy, since Dom had fully outgrown what was available at his preschool. Today, on the way to his parents' home to begin a long weekend break from his sophomore year in college, Dom decided to pay Mrs. Kennedy a visit.

Once inside the school, Dom was inspired to take a nostalgic, meandering route to her office. Along the way, he noticed that the band room was now half of what used to be an auditorium, and that the third graders were located on a totally different floor. He soon arrived at the Hub, a circular space that a few hallways were connected to, and which was still being used for general, mixed-use seating.

Dom had fond memories of this spot, he had burned dozens of half hours after art classes poring over sketch pads or clay blocks, waiting for one of his parents to pick him up. He had never actually seen it in normal day use and was surprised to find a couple dozen kids of varying ages making use of it: a group of popular girls giggling, a trio of boys plus one girl playing a board game, single kids scattered throughout with books and worksheets. And then, as expected, one small boy toiling away with a pen, hunched over a drawing, several other art utensils at his side. He was humbly dressed, assumedly not "of" the more well-to-do families that dominated the area. Dom grinned and watched the artist for several seconds, then started to continue on his way when a new development slowed his pace.

A much larger boy approached the same table from behind the artist's view, reaching down with his right hand to clasp the latter's neck, tightly enough to cause the smaller boy to clench his shoulders and drop his pen. Without releasing his grip, the larger kid sat down to the artist's left and leaned in, clearly harassing the smaller victim. Dom was angry. He zeroed in with his eyes and calmly stepped down two stairs into the Hub.

The room became quieter as half of the other Hub occupants stopped what they were doing to check out what this tall, skinny, odd-looking teenager was doing in their space, walking with purpose and a fixed gaze. Without saying a word, Dom stepped over the bench of the table where the boys were sitting and sat to the left of the bully. For several seconds, the larger boy obliviously continued his harassment, the other boy's neck still in his grip, shaking the latter as he dropped nasty, threatening remarks.

"I will fuckin' kick your smelly little ass if-..." Something in the back of the bully's mind had registered an atmospheric change that was crystallized when his left leg brushed against Dom's. He turned, puzzled, quickly raising his head as he realized that a large adult was sitting beside him all of a sudden, staring straight ahead at the blank wall opposite their position at the table. The boy's jaw slackened, his grip loosened, then Dom slowly turned to look at the boy, who was frozen in shock. Dom's eyes were wide, intently staring with an otherwise blank expression at the bully.

Ever so quietly, Dom asked, "What do you think you're doing?"

The boy paused before stammering back, "Uh... n- nothin'."

"Nothin'?" Dom asked.

"No, uh. I wasn't... doin' nothin'. I was just..."

Dom held up a long index finger to halt the boy's excuse. "I don't think it was nothin'. I think... it was SOMETHING." This last word he emphasized in a deeper voice through clenched teeth, tilting his head down toward the boy. He clamped his jaws in a way he knew would make his cheeks and temples flare.

By this point the smaller boy was also watching Dom with wide eyes, not yet understanding that he was being rescued. The larger boy remained motionless. Dom hoped he wasn't pissing his pants.

After a few more seconds of the stare-down, Dom quietly said, still in his deep intimidation voice, "Apologize."

"I'm sorry," the boy immediately responded.

Dom stifled a grin. "Not to me."

"Oh. Oh," the boy said, then turned just briefly toward the smaller boy before quickly flicking his head back on Dom again, then, satisfied that Dom probably wasn't going to eat him, turned once again to his victim and said, "I'm sorry, Ben."

Ben was still taken aback by the situation and continued looking up at Dom. A moment passed before he looked over at his attacker. "Oh," he said. "Okay."

The larger boy turned apprehensively back at Dom again.

Still imposingly locking eyes with the kid, Dom took a deep breath and said, "Now go away."

"Okay." The boy wasted no time jumping up over the bench and running out of the Hub, tripping on the top step before escaping around a hallway corner, sneaking one last glance back at Dom before he did so.

Dom watched the bully until he disappeared, then turn his gaze back to the artist, who was still staring wide-eyed back at him. Dom grinned and lightly chuckled. "You're welcome," he said in a more normal voice.

Ben smiled back unsteadily and said, "Oh, thanks."

Dom looked down at the sketchbook in front of Ben. "Watcha workin' on?"

Ben, still a bit stunned looked down at the book and said, "Uh, a baby dragon." He handed the sketchbook to Dom.

Dom hadn't originally been able to see the kid's work, he had been standing too far away. So he was pleasantly surprised to discover, as he quietly evaluated the drawing, that it was worth evaluation. He quickly moved past the drawing in progress and surveyed the rest of the sketchbook. The breadth of experiments in color, texture, and medium were impressive in their own right — clearly the kid was on a learning streak — but the finesse of the lines really spoke to Dom, they showed actual skill and style. Ben appeared to really care about his craft.

He closed the sketchbook, silently contemplated for a moment, then turned to the boy and stoically, meaningfully said, "These are really good." Ben had visibly become concerned by Dom's initial lack of a response, but now flashed a relieved smile. Dom paused and looked back down at the book, feeling a connection to his earlier days and a sudden (almost uncomfortable) kinship with the boy. Finally, he faced Ben again, held out the sketchbook and said, "Keep at it. This is important."

The boy seemed awestruck by Dom's sincerity, the smile fading as he looked down and gently took the book. "Okay," he said, looking back up at Dom again. "I will. Thanks."

Dom threw Ben a sly smile, stood, and left.

Due diligence required that the state confirm with Dominic Winters that he had harbored no intention of luring depressed street urchins to their deaths with his gruesome creation (and he was, fortunately, collected enough to say so via notarized letter), but the criminal case was officially over when Grace Adkins quietly but emphatically told the district attorney to forget about it. Whatever white trash algorithm that she and her current common-law husband had used in the weighing of monetary outcomes determined that burying Lee's death in service of Daniel's eventual fame was preferable to suing the bejesus out of a famous but not yet wealthy artist.

The family and authorities would thus be held at bay, but the community would not...

"Winters is a KILLER. He knew what he was doing, he *knew* someone would want to kill themself on that awful, evil thing. We want him and his death chair out of our town!" This brief rant, one of the first to punctuate the local news reports on the protests against Dom Winters and *The Conclusion*, reasonably summed up the feelings of the Cape residents. The underlying message, though, was that the art school itself was unwanted. A war was brewing.

"Look, I'm not going to say that the chair wasn't risky." Also frequently represented in the media frenzy were members of the art school student body, who were now caught in the crossfire, whether they wanted to be or not, and whether or not they had any firsthand knowledge of Dom or his creation. One student's sound bite had been used on most of the local reports as a catch-all summary of the feelings on campus. "Its whole reason for being is violent suicide. But are you really going to persecute one person for creating his version of a death machine when half of the families in this county own *shotguns?*" This increasingly bandied-about question was arguably fair and unquestionably inflammatory, and it only furthered to divide the two factions.

The treatment of the story by media varied depending on its origin; the local stations tended to favor the feelings of the community, while the national news generally sided with the art community in defending Dom (Fox News being, predictably, the one exception). Because voices on both sides of the fence varied widely in logic and articulateness, it was easy to promote one view over the other by way of selective broadcasting. Whether or not the tragedy merited international attention, it was a gold mine for the news industry.

His mother may have been content to leave the incident alone, but the neighbors who had consistently ignored Lee in life were now embracing him postmortem. A pixelated enlargement of his expressionless yearbook photo (the only picture the public had access to, since Grace Adkins and what remained of her family had gone into hiding) was emblazoned on posters and picket signs everywhere, often side by side with one of the comparatively easily to access photos of Dom, who of course had appeared in glossy publications all over the world in the months after *the Conclusion* made its debut. The unusually shaped sculpture was difficult to depict clearly on such a display, but another frequently used icon in the protest campaign was the arrow-with-a-hole silhouette that the chair's back formed, usually accompanied by an exaggerated representation of the coil/spike apparatus underneath it. Malevolent intent or no, it was not difficult to portray Dominic Winters and his machine as willing harbingers of death; the palpable fear on which the piece was based was the same fear that played into the embittered and paranoid hearts of the Cape Johns working class.

Things devolved at a rapid pace. With such potent figureheads cleanly dividing two such diametrically opposed schools of thought, tensions rose exponentially. The town of Cape Johns had for some time been primed for an explosion, and Lee's suicide was ten times the catalyst needed to finally pull the trigger. Vitriol turned to violence eight days after *the Conclusion* unleashed its wrath.

"Bob, I'm standing outside of St. Vincent Hospital, where CJAI student Brian Edwards lies in intensive care after suffering multiple stab wounds at the hands of two local bar patrons..." Evan Johns turned the volume down and stared with a heavy heart at the blurry screen of Alex's ancient 13" TV. He closed his eyes and massaged his aching forehead, then let out a long, deep sigh.

Alex walked in from his bedroom. He had just left Dom, who was finally asleep after another 20-hour period of restless despondence.

"Oh shit." Any semblance of relief over Dom's nap was yanked away by images of police tape and ambulances on the screen. "What happened?"

Johns reopened his eyes and stared back at the screen. "You don't want to know. And neither does Dom," he said quietly before gazing vacantly into the blue sky out the window. "But this is going to get worse before it gets better, Alex. Try as we might, we are not going to be able to keep Dom in the dark. I don't like to think what... he..." He paused in thought, then turned to face Alex, sharing an ashen, bloodshot gaze for several seconds. "I don't know what to do."

Dom's nightmares took different forms, but they always told the same basic story. The happy moments were brief, as though the mind was saying, "Okay, enough of that, you know what we're here to see."

This time the setting was an exotic evening party in New York under a massive canvas tent, Dom was wearing a sharp grey suit with a bright white dress shirt, posted in a throne-like chair on a dais above the surrounding crowd, flanked by sinewy, bronzed women. Stilted, elusive music permeated the air while floor performers of different types entertained the crowd: a juggler, a four-legged acrobat, a woman with flaming limbs. Dom was grinning, coolly absorbing his lofty position in such a resplendent crowd.

Across the room, near a side exit, wearing tattered, Mad Max-ian clothing and carrying a golden scimitar, Eddie appeared. He was the only person in the room not smiling until he was noticed by Dom. Dom's euphoria fell, just before Alex appeared at his side, wearing a khaki uniform. He leaned down toward Dom's ear and half-whispered something that Dom couldn't understand. Dom tried to wave him off, still fixated on the danger that the new intruder posed, but Alex tugged at Dom's arm, insistent. Dom finally looked at Alex, who was waving and pointing behind the dais, now becoming frantic. Dom willed his chair to swivel to the other direction and the scene went dark.

The music vanished in an instant, leaving behind an almost vacuum-like silence. The surroundings were now nearly all black, save for a dim, blurred walkway that appeared in front of his throne, which was now just a wooden chair. Dom realized he was wearing a pair of scruffy yellow overalls, and his hands were scarred and callused. He looked in all directions for Alex or anyone else, but saw no one. The walkway seemed to be the only option, so he stood up from the chair and started cautiously walking forward.

A faint but haunting wail emanated from the distance, just as a warm breeze glanced across Dom's face. He was carefully focused on following the walkway, which now felt more like a tenuous bridge. His heart rate increased. Without realizing it, he was clenching his jaw, and after several steps, he felt one of his molars shatter under the pressure. He stopped, reached inside his mouth and pulled out the remnants of the bloody tooth, then carefully put them in his pocket. His body started to shake. Dom reached into his mouth again and felt his other teeth, which all seemed to be loose, on the verge of falling out. He started to panic, breathing rapidly, when he noticed the muffled sound of footsteps. He held is breath to listen. Someone was approaching.

Dom hunched down and peered down the grey path into the blackness, his deteriorated mouth hanging open, panting. The footsteps continued their march, loud wooden knocks against a hollow floor. Whoever was approaching should have been right in front of him by now, and Dom crouched even lower in anticipation. A sudden realization set in, and with a jolt of fear, he rose and turned to face the other direction to find Lee Adkins — or some portion of him — staring wide-eyed back at him.

Dom inhaled suddenly in shock before he paused and looked more carefully, suddenly wondering if this meant that Lee was still alive. But no, a casual glance downward removed any doubt: supporting the head was a shrivel of a torso, nothing that could be called human.

Dom looked back up to the face, where Lee's lips parted, slowly, and a dark rushing sound of wind emanated from his mouth. Rivulets of oily fluid streamed horizontally out of the corners, reaching the back of his jaw before dripping backward into space on either side of his head, as though gravity ran parallel to the floor.

Dom stood rigid in confusion and fear. He heard a slight semblance of a boy's moaning voice before the top half of Lee's head swung slowly backward before ripping across the cheeks, as though hinged at the back of the neck, then suddenly separating entirely and tumbling backward into the blackness. Dom screamed "NO!" and lunged forward to desperately grasp for the disembodied skull, reaching over the shoulder of, and colliding with, what was left of Lee's cold, wet, now headless body.

The head had vanished into the violet and blue fog receding into the distance, and realizing that he was making contact with the haunting corpse, Dom pushed away from it in shocked revulsion. The still-connected lower jaw turned and swung downward with the rest of the carcass while black liquid spewed out from the neck, forming a weightless, geyser-like arc in the air over Dom's head.

By this point, Dom was distraught to the point of collapse, and with strained face and tears flowing, he let loose a final, barely recognizable "NO!" before waking himself up in a sweat of convulsions.

"We want it destroyed." Local dock worker union boss Amos Miller was being interviewed by Steve Kroft in a 60 Minutes segment about the controversy (much of the atmospheric footage for the piece had been shot weeks earlier as a feature on Dom and his chair, shortly before Lee's death). Miller had risen to become the spearhead voice for the campaign against Winters's "abomination" (now referred to as the "Chuck the Chair" movement, or CTC). He was a burly, stoic man who was used to addressing large groups and people in power, and his interactions made it clear that he was intimidated by no one. "It's just that simple, Steve. We don't want Mr. Winters's head on a stick. We don't want to burn the art school down. We *do* feel that this chair has no place in a world already riddled with problems. It is a symbol of death and despair, and we want it destroyed."

That sound bite was the whole of Miller's appearance in nationally syndicated media, but he had a much larger footprint in local and regional media. Worldwide, the argument may have been socially relevant, but in Cape Johns, it was personal.

"ARREST THAT ASSHOLE!" These were the sorts of impassioned, short-fuse comments that Amos Miller wished his flock would keep to themselves; keeping the CTC's message dignified was a constant battle due to the smoldering anger that lay beneath its surface. He had just been introduced by a protest organizer and was approaching the podium to speak to a crowd of roughly one hundred locals in front of the museum that continued to display *The Conclusion* under heavy guard. A phalanx of expressionless police officers stood between the speaking platform and the restless crowd, ready to do battle if the situation got out of hand, but hopelessly outnumbered if it did.

Miller quieted the crowd with calm hand gestures, then rested his palms on the podium and paused for dramatic effect before speaking, in an oaken voice, slowly and directly into as many pairs of eyes as his time allowed. "This... is not... a war. This is not an inquisition, my friends. But this *is* a call to duty. We... you and I... represent the backbone of this town, of this region. I don't think we ask for much. I don't think we overstep our bounds. I think we do a good job of respecting the lives of those who reside here temporarily, for they too are an integral part of *any* thriving community." The crowd vocally, if not emphatically, cheered approval. He was subtly informing the crowd of what he wanted to be true, not entirely what was. He paused again, taking a deep breath, then reached into the interior pocket of his wool coat. "But this...." He pulled out a glossy photo of the chair. *"This...* goes too far." A more enthusiastic response this time. "This... piece of... art..." Belly-laughs from the audience. "The legitimacy of it may be in question, but the safety of an object like this in our community is not. We're workin' hard to stay afloat, folks, and some of us aren't coping as well as others. The *last* thing we need... is an invitation to end it all!" Passionate cheers throughout.

Three attempts to steal or destroy the piece had been made so far, two of them clumsy and easily thwarted, one of them well-planned and nearly successful. In a Hollywood-esque operation conducted by members of the CTC faithful, a team of crafty would-be thieves first contacted the evening cleaning company to cancel that night's shift — citing a special "security exercises" session — then impersonated the same with great care, mimicking everything from the white and blue company van to the laminated security badges that one of the team had covertly snapped photos of the week before. They were thwarted only by their incomplete knowledge of the museum's security measures; the two extra guards who stood watch *inside* the chair's actual display room were a new addition that the CTC's intel hadn't included. So instead of defacing the chair on-site with cloaked torches and rotary saws, they nervously cleaned much of the museum before slipping out and escaping in the van. No one on the museum staff knew anything had happened until the cleaning company called to ask if they should resume their duties the following night.

No one died. That would be the only positive spin one could put on the most violent civil altercation Cape Johns had seen since the Vietnam War. No one died, but roughly three dozen were injured, five of them seriously. It started in the Downs.

Just as first-time-wealthy lottery winners are magnetically drawn back to their native economic class, kids like Bobby Childress are drawn to the edgy no-man's-land of the Downs, whose isolated environment allowed him to stretch his inner city legs a bit — getting high, spray-painting or destroying walls here and there, creating a bonfire or two before getting chased away by police or school security. He had merged into an existing group of kids with a similar past, a couple of whom were actually Cape locals (another was Eddie Carrick).

Bobby had meandered over to the Downs after a tense private confrontation with a sculpture teacher who made little secret of his disdain for Bobby's presence. Thanks to some effective counseling, the stoic but intense student had recently been learning to appreciate the power he gained by taking the high road during such events, and it was only by clinging fiercely to that lesson that he was able to maintain composure and walk away before lashing out. That tension and anger was still bubbling under the surface, however, when three Cape hoodlums caught site of him relaxing on the patio of a former Downs studio, smoking a cigarette in the evening sun.

"Well, well. An art school faggot." The assumed leader of the trio stepped confidently into the patio space with the others falling into place on either side. He was lanky but tall, with olive skin, dark, spiked hair and a flawed smile. The other two were shorter but stockier, and neither of them were smiling. The leader's smiled faded a bit, then he calmly said, "You got a cigarette for me, art fag?"

Bobby had been internally startled by the sudden presence of the gang, but his fixed stare on the tall one never gave that away. After several seconds, he calmly puffed a cloud of smoke toward the group and said, "Sure do. Why don't you come over here and get it?"

The tall one smiled a bit more, with just a bit less confidence than before, then tilted his head downward and sauntered over toward Bobby. He stopped about two feet short of Bobby's seated position.

The others remained in place twelve feet away. Quietly, he said, "let's have it, tough guy."

Bobby glanced back up at him, took a deep breath, reached down to put out his cigarette on the floor, then casually scooped up a handful of dusty sand from the floor with his (non-dominant) right hand and threw it upward into his opponent's face. In a fraction of a second, Bobby met the hood's lowered, cringing, blinded face with a well-anchored left-hand uppercut fueled by several months of suppressed anger. His victim barely had time to fall to the floor, unconscious and dropping a trail of blood from his nose and mouth, before his friends lunged forward to take over the fight.

Most of the art school was bordered either by lilting, well-manicured natural spaces, or by expansive parking lots and garages. These provided a much-needed buffer between the commingled but disparate worlds, allowing students and locals to go about their days without having to be confronted by the presence of one another. But in the northwestern corner of the rounded rectangle of the school grounds lay a large, dilapidated expanse borne of a failed vision of integration.

Professor Samuel Barnett studied sociology before migrating to his second love, impressionist painting, in the hopes that he might merge the two to form a new kind of society-lifting academic discipline. He toiled in his studies for most of the 1950's, never to be taken very seriously by either field. But his hope for a harmonious society never wavered, especially in the face of the increasingly divided Cape Johns community.

Barnett found a new vehicle for his dream in a school-adjacent plot of land abandoned by an auto parts factory and snapped up by the school's board of directors before any of the local businesses were able to get their act together. The board had primarily sought to expand the school's footprint to account for future growth and had no immediate use for the land itself. Barnett did.

After a great deal of pleading to an unsympathetic but weary school board, Barnett was allowed a meager commission to build his new dream: the Cape Johns Unification of Spirit Downs. "The Downs," as the space was henceforth known, was intended to be a beautifully-manicured community space that would bridge the gap between the two worlds. In its rudimentary, adobe-style studios, free art classes would be taught by volunteers and graduate students to Cape residents of any age. It was a beautiful sentiment that died a quick death in the face of major obstacles: overworked student teachers resented being forced to deal with antagonistic local teens booted into the classes by lazy parents and social workers; the volunteer teaching and management backbone never surfaced; and the bare-minimum project budget never produced the serene landscaping that Barnett's vision relied on. The professor remained the Downs's most ardent supporter until faced with the bleak reality, five years into the project, that the wasteland it had become would never be revived. He retired shortly thereafter, never to return to the school.

Today, the Downs stands as the school's embarrassing secret that no one on the board wants to address: a dusty, barren back-lot, riddled with a few crumbling, graffiti-covered classrooms and surrounded by barbed chain-link fences (and mostly blocked from the students' view by a twelve-foot hedge). Many half-hearted attempts had been made — usually by freshman board members — to transform the eyesore into something useful, but the space's proximity to a vengeful Cape neighborhood always won out. The space could not be safely occupied by students, storage or infrastructure. Nonetheless, it was occupied by both students and locals on the evening of April 12th.

Bobby Childress might have ended up on either side of that fence. Though artistically gifted, he had been in and out of juvenile correction due to the abuse he forwarded from his alcoholic father to his peers. He wound up on the lucky side of a judge's decision to either A) hand Bobby to an inner-city scholarship program designed to pull youths out of their broken pasts, or B) send the now of-age Bobby to jail. In a state with less crowded prisons, the conservative judge might have opted for the latter, but instead he opted to give the scholarship program the benefit of the doubt. Bobby was shipped from his native Queens, NY to Cape Johns, and he had kept his temper more or less in check for most of his first year. But that was about to change.

Bobby and his newer opponents made enough ruckus to draw the attention of two school-affiliated hoods who were drinking nearby. They rounded the corner to catch the two townies, one of whom was already bloody from his nose to his chest, relentlessly pounding the now-struggling Bobby just outside of the building's doorway. Immediately they dove in and rescued him, while he fell to his hands and knees and crawled into the empty classroom to get his bearings.

Things escalated quickly from there, the brawl attracting more and more bodies until it formed a field battle of nearly forty young men. Some of them were knocked unconscious, a few were mercilessly beaten on the ground and several fled the scene before a dozen squad cars surrounded the area and rushed in to drop the hammer on the fracas. When all was said and done, twenty-three kids were arrested, seventeen sent to the hospital, and one Robert Julian Childress wound up in the ICU with three broken ribs and massive internal bleeding. He would emerge three weeks later with only one functioning eye.

No one died. But the town was in shock. The chaotic violence may have had nothing to do with Dom's chair, but it didn't matter. Kids from both sides of the divide going to the hospital ensured that the intensity and participation in the burgeoning civil war would increase.

Art school president Jonathan Eckler stepped calmly in front of the podium and paused for a few seconds while camera flashes died down and video equipment settled. He was a quiet, dignified man in his early sixties who wore glasses, a neatly trimmed beard and a light gray suit. Looking down at the prepared statement in his hand, he took a breath and spoke in a deep, neutral tone. "It is with deep regret that I must inform the students and faculty of the Cape Johns School of Art that the campus must be temporarily closed and the premises vacated." He paused while a flurry of conversation subsided. "Tensions surrounding the death of Lee Adkins and the recent violence at the Unification Downs leave us no other choice. We must act in the best interest of our students' and faculty members' safety, and there are simply too many indicators of potential further bloodshed..."

"Dom!" Karen quickly turned off the TV as soon as he appeared in the doorway, but it was too late. He had already heard what was happening and continued to stare at the blank screen, ignoring Karen, who sat with a distraught look on her face, not sure what to do. He stood rigid and motionless, at the same time furious and lost.

Dom spoke sharply without averting his gaze. "What happened at the Downs?"

"Nothing that had anything to do with y-..."

"How could it fucking NOT have anything to do with me?!" Dom cried through bloodshot eyes, now facing Karen with arms taught and fists clenched. "Violence at the Downs, enough to shut the entire fucking SCHOOL down? When the fuck has that ever happened, Karen, *when*?"

Karen stood calmly, trying to avoid letting tension hanging in the air rise further. She took a breath and opened her mouth, about to recite the agreed-upon story. But Dom clearly wasn't going to buy it anymore, maintaining a level "try me" stare.

Then something shifted in her. Her demeanor shifted, and she stared flatly into his eyes. "All right Dom," she said. "You created a poison pill. The chair you built set this town off, it finally broke the *thin* barrier that... that was keeping the townies from slaughtering us all. Maybe if a kid in that terrible state hadn't-..."

"His name is Lee," Dom interjected abruptly.

Karen nodded. "Of course. If *Lee* hadn't gained illegal access to... the chair... then maybe none of this would have happened. *Maybe.*"

Dom held up a hand to pause her speech, then spoke quietly, slowly through mournful, bloodshot eyes, "But it did happen."

Karen took a deep breath again and simply held space for a moment, staring into Dom's face, trying to bleed away as much of his torment as she could. After several seconds she spoke again. "You created a work of *art* that a lot of people didn't understand. How could you have known that... all of this *shit* would happen?" Her voice fell. "Dom," she said gently, lovingly, "why is any of this your fault?"

For the briefest of moments, the argument gave Dom pause. But his face quickly returned to that of consternation. "No. I'm not blind, Karen, I know the internal rage of this town as well as anyone. But I *was* blind... during my moment of 'epiphany.' During my moment of power. If I had just thought about the possible consequences..." A tear fell from one eye. "I should have known."

Karen wasn't having it, she shook her head. "We all felt that rage and none of us guessed that this would happen, Dom. We gladly supported you, we celebrated the meaning of the chair..."

"You followed me because you believed in *me* and you knew the depths that I was coming from." Dom's tone was shifting from morose to angry. He fixated on Karen's eyes. "I led you with my blind ego, every one of you." He turned to look out the window.

That viewpoint didn't land well. Karen responded in a frank tone. "You... *led* us? We weren't your followers, we aren't blind, and you're not omniscient, Mister Winters. It's easy to see it that way in hindsight, but I strongly disagree that any of us, including you, could have predicted this cause and effect relationship." She leaned in front of him so that he looked her in the eye. "It's *not* your fault. It's not."

Dom let out a breath and his gaze drifted downward. He whispered, "Okay," and stood lifelessly. Karen stepped forward and gently pushed her arms under his, and around his back, embracing him firmly with her head on his chest, eyes closed. Dom loosely laid his arms over her, but felt nothing, staring through the apartment door into a void.

As is common during a period of depression, Dom's physical condition added to his snowball effect of self-loathing. He didn't care to keep himself presentable, and his ever-devolving appearance only served to lower his spirits further. That phenomenon aside, Dom hadn't had the will or bravery to look at himself in the mirror for nearly two weeks. So when he inadvertently caught his reflection while closing the medicine cabinet, the image he confronted was a shock to an already shocked system.

Briefly, he was mesmerized. Dom had simply never looked this neglected before in his life, and to gaze upon a visage so perfectly *bad* fascinated him utterly. It was like a candy store for the artistically-trained eye, he didn't know what to study first: skin with the pallor of an addict but the oily glow of an expectant mother; blood-ringed eyes framed by bags that could have been applied with theater makeup; a gradient of dark, glistening, unkempt facial hair ranging from gnat-sized stubs at his cheekbones to a malformed jungle at his jaw-line. Unapologetic nose hairs. Chapped lips. Yellowing teeth. Crusty, infected earring. It was a composition of grim reality that many artists would love to capture.

But the fascination came to an abrupt end when Dom remembered that he was looking at himself, and why his appearance had come to this. The Great Dominic Winters, inadvertent murderer. Suddenly he glared with contempt. "You," he said quietly to himself. "Fucking imposter." His hatred of that face burned in his chest and neck. "Awful... worthless..." His eyes widened, his pulse and breath shot up. "DOG SHIT!" he yelled at the top of his lungs before throwing his entire body behind a furious right-hand punch into the mirror, which caved in like a paper sack, throwing bits of glass all over Dom's body and the bathroom floor, and large shards onto the basin below.

Breathing heavily, head buzzing with energy, gazing first at the dented rectangle of tin frame that desperately held to the cabinet in front of him, now encircled with barely-clinging glass shards, Dom's head fell downward until he caught site of his hand, which, for the second time in less than a year, was covered in fresh blood. The shock of the past minute was quickly giving way to a swarm of searing pain all over his hand. Dom's mind battled against itself — hating himself versus not caring about anything at all versus an injury that would not be ignored. The former feelings put up a valiant effort, but the pain was going to win. It was unbearable.

Wincing, barely perceiving his world in this moment, he stepped around the corner to the linen closet, unfolded a clean hand towel and gingerly laid his hand onto it, folding its top and sides inward and around. Returning to the glass-riddled bathroom, he was able to find medical tape in a basin drawer, which he used to secure the makeshift bandage, now rapidly turning red with seeping blood.

This task completed, Dom wasn't sure what to do with himself. He sat on the toilet seat for just a few seconds before standing up quickly and walking into the hall, where he stopped, looked toward the living room, then back toward the bedrooms, and back again. He walked slowly into the living room and looked around, listless, confused, trying to ignore the throbbing of his wounds. Dom stood still for a full minute, lazily scanning the room and waiting for inspiration — what now? — but none came. And since nothing in his environment provided an escape, the emotions of his reality began to surface.

They were complex, and in conflict with one another. Part of Dom's being needed very much to cry, to mourn his predicament, to release a well of shunned pain much deeper than that which his flesh currently offered. Equally urgent was a charge of furious anger, both at himself and at the talent that put him here. He mentally bounced back and forth between the two, achieving nothing but an increased heart rate and rapid breathing, almost to the brink of passing out. He slowly, lightly crumbled to the floor, gazing in tormented disorientation directly at the foot of a wooden coffee table that was pushing a depression into Karen's cheap, lime green acrylic carpet. When only the anxiety and heavy breathing remained, he whimpered a bit, then tried a scream. But neither satisfied his opposing needs. He was locked in place. Dom rolled gently to the floor and relaxed a bit, still staring at the table leg.

He was at his wit's end. There was simply no escape from the situation, it felt as though the entire world had surrounded his thin walls, brandishing torches and pitchforks. Early the following morning, after a typically restless night, Dom could think of only one possible respite from the brutal chaos that engulfed his life: Ferron Tower. The glorious bird's eye view that had so often given him an avenue for letting go might just be the only place where he could get some distance from his problems. If he could set all of this aside, just for a moment...

There just wasn't anything else. He had to try.

Dom quietly dressed, gingerly favoring his injured right hand. Closing the front door, he turned to face the grey, cool morning of the urban-rural border of the Cape Johns south side, where industry and commerce tapered off in favor of dingy, ancient row houses. Not much was stirring. For a moment Dom felt relieved; he was outside for the first time in almost a week, and didn't have to encounter anyone who would recognize him.

But better safe than sorry, and Dom pulled out from his right coat pocket, using his undamaged left hand, a dark winter cap that would hopefully allow him to blend in with the rising townies while he made his way to the tower. He walked down the path through Karen's short front yard, stepped left and stopped. He realized that he was carrying no art supplies. No pencils. No paper. This plan could not succeed without those tools.

The art supply stores were out of the question. If anyone was going to recognize and attempt to interact with Dom, it would be the art store employees, most of whom were fellow students. And they would still be closed anyway. But hell, were "real" supplies crucial here? Dom resolved to make his way to the grungiest dime store or gas station he could find.

Karl's Korner seemed appropriate, a tiny bodega with barely-functioning signs and an overall dirty complexion. And although it was apparently open, no one could be seen entering or exiting. Dom walked in with his head down.

"Mornin'!" greeted a chipper shopkeeper from behind the counter. Dom turned just enough to grunt a reply without looking at the man and kept moving forward toward a rack of miscellany. There he found a stack of navy blue pencils and a stack of ruled, hole-punched note pads. Not exactly a master's toolbox, but it would do. He grabbed two of each and walked to the front.

"Kinda grim out there today, eh?" The man — assumedly, this was Karl — seemed intent on striking up a friendly chat.

"Yep," Dom replied in a noncommittal deadpan that suggested he wasn't interested in playing. He pulled out his wallet as the man casually rang up the items.

"I think I'd rather it rained than stay this drizzly all the time." Dom finally looked up enough to see the man's friendly smile. He was graying and middle-aged, with a peppered mustache and metal-rimmed glasses. "You heading for the morning shift, or coming off the night shift?"

Dom grinned despite himself, both because of the absurdity of the man's question, relative to Dom's current situation, and of the man's apparent lack of recognition of one of the most talked about men in the country. "Morning shift," he answered quietly.

"Ah. Well, have a good one," the man answered back with a thumbs-up.

Dom nodded back, and turned to walk out, tucking the tools under his arm, when he realized that the pencils hadn't been sharpened yet. He stopped at the doorway and took a deep breath, then slowly turned back toward the shopkeeper with one of the pencils upturned in his non-injured hand. "Um..."

"Oh, here, I'll take care of it," said the man, waving Dom back to the counter before Dom could even ask for help. Dom walked back and handed the pencil over as the man pulled out a pocket knife and deftly whittled the pencil's tip to a point. He started to hand the pencil back to Dom, but pulled it back momentarily. "Hmmm... not going to get very far with just that. Let's see..." He stepped back from his counter, opened a drawer and rummaged through it.

Dom was leery of waiting any longer. "Um, it's okay, I think..."

"No, no, I've got something in here... ah!" He held up a tiny, Swiss Army-style pocketknife with a worn dry cleaning logo on it. "Let's make sure you don't get stuck with any more non-writing sticks," he said, still grinning, and handed both over to Dom.

"That's..." Dom paused, a bit taken aback by the man's kindness and generosity. It had been awhile since he had received either of those things from a stranger. "That's really kind of you. Thank you," he said back quietly. He held up the pencil and knife in thanks again before turning and walking back to the front door.

"Mister... Winters?" the man called to him. Dom froze. He stood for a moment, staring at the ground outside the doorway, then slowly turned to face the man, who was no longer smiling. The man stared for a moment, then said quietly, somewhat self-consciously, "I... I love your work."

Dom stood in shock, not knowing what to do, eyes locked with the shopkeeper. After several tense moments, he nodded, almost imperceptibly, and walked briskly out the door.

Any pleasantness engendered by the dewy, sparsely-populated morning and cheerful, helpful stranger had been dashed by the realization that the latter had recognized him. Even at the darkest hour, in the dingiest corner, there didn't seem to be any escape from his reality.

Just get to the tower, that's all Dom needed to do right now. He kept his head down and walked at a brisk pace, turning his coat collar up high and keeping a shadowed eye out for other people, doing his best to give a wide berth to the few who were out.

Twenty minutes later, he was at the tower's base. The rusty, green and heavily-locked front gate had always been something of a joke, since the poorly-designed entrance left an easy-to-circumvent side area for anyone with a modicum of athleticism to slip through. Still, making that passage with an essentially useless dominant hand was tricky. Dom struggled a bit to manage it with his three healthy limbs, but made it to the other side with just a light bruise on his upper right arm.

The rest of the ascent was comparatively easy, including only a couple of jumps over faulty or missing stair steps. Dom was starting to feel desperate to reach the top by now and panted as he jogged up the last few stairs. The morning had started to clear several minutes ago, and now the Cape harbour was once again clad in full golden regalia.

Dom took a deep breath and surveyed his surroundings in admiration. Tears welled in his eyes. He remembered with a twinge of heartache his last journey to this perch, just before the cliff accident. Then the street attack. And the thoughts of suicide. And Lee's death. Is that all that was left for Dom in this life? Darkness and pain?

He shook his head free of those thoughts and breathed deeply. No more dwelling, it was time to escape into the paper. Dom assumed his usual seat, a crude concrete bench connected to the metal frame of the tower's apex, pulled out the sharpened pencil and a pad. He took another deep breath and stared, pencil in hand, at the blank sheet in his lap.

Nothing came out. No obvious subjects or scenes materialized. Dom surveyed the scene in front of him but could concentrate on nothing. No degree of glimmering morning glory could distract him from the guilt and pain that burned him through. Every attempt to render what lay before him was thwarted by an equal absence of concentration and interest. As frantically as he made his way to this hopeful point of salvation, as deeply as he *needed* to forget, even for a moment, what his brilliantly deadly creation had made of him, he could do nothing but hurt. If ever Dom had longed for unfortunate events to bestow divine inspiration upon him, he now needed more than anything to make them disappear. Yet again, he crumpled in torment, silent tears dropping onto the empty canvas.

And then... something flipped over in Dom's mind. He lifted his head and stared out onto the shimmering water and reached the second most important decision of his life. He slowly stood up, growing more sure as he rose of what he knew he had to do. The wind was crisp and sobering, drying away his tears. A determined chuckle, the first in several weeks, forced itself out, and a slight grin turned up the corner of his mouth. He looked down at the pad and pencil in his hands, and, without thinking, wrote down three words, giggling despite himself, tore off the paper they were written on, folded and stuffed it in his breast pocket. Then another deep breath. He bent over to lay the pad and pencil down on the bench, then rose, eyes raw and alive, again taking in his surroundings, appreciating this moment: cool morning air, golden-grey sky, sounds of ships and cars peppered with the cries of seagulls.

He took a step forward to the guard railing, placing his hands on the top rail, then stepped up onto the middle bar, leaning with his shins against the top. Quietly, he recited a verse from his favorite poem:

Magnanimous Despair alone
Could show me so divine a thing
Where feeble Hope could ne'er have flown,
But vainly flapp'd its tinsel wing.

Upon finishing the verse, realizing that it had never contained any specific meaning for him until this moment, he laughed again through tears, then sobbed deeply into his hands, stepping back down to the platform, finally releasing the pain he had been carrying for so long.

Regaining his composure, Dom took a breath and stepped up to the middle bar once more, then again onto the top rail before crouching down and touching the rail beside his feet. Then, with a graceful motion he had so frequently practiced before gracelessly landing in a treasured blue-green pond, leaped forward with all of his might. The apex seemed to go on forever this time. He thought of his mother, with feelings of longing and a pang of regret. Then he fell, arcing forward slowly. In his most daring moments Dom had never jumped from half this height, and the louder-than-life wind buffeting across his ears seemed the perfect build-up to what would presently be the grand crescendo of his life. It would all be over soon. It was over.

life

"What are you thinking?"

Alex and Karen sat on a bench facing a construction site that would soon be the Dominic Winters Memorial Building. It would primarily be used as studio space for fine arts graduates.

"I'm trying not to," Alex said, watching the autumn leaves blow across the solidified mud that was the building's future front lawn. "It's just going to take awhile for my life to... re-center itself, I guess."

Karen solemnly pondered that. "Dom was the center of all of our lives in one way or another."

They sat in silence for several minutes. "Alex," Karen finally said. "Is it enough? Would this have satisfied him?"

Alex considered it for a moment and said, "This... this stuff is irrelevant — he wouldn't really care about a building. The notoriety, respect... I think that's what he cared about, and he got that." Karen put her head on his shoulder. "Short as his story may be, it's definitely in the books." He brushed a tear away before it had a chance to run down his cheek.

"Good riddance, we don't need him or his trash" was one of the few remaining hateful Caper quotes published after Dom's death. The tensions coursing through the town largely died down in the weeks following Dom's suicide. Benefiting this peaceful shift was the temporary transfer of the chair to the MOMA in New York City, who insisted on leaving the chair's spring and spike in their expanded state rather than compress it again (which, besides making it safer, had the important side benefit of demonstrating its history; it had not been touched, save for cleaning, since taking Lee's life). Anti-chair leader

Amos Miller issued one last statement to the press before dissolving the Chuck the Chair organization:

"Five years will not be enough. If the late Mr. Winters' chair shows up again on Cape Johns soil, our protests will be renewed and redoubled. We don't want the chair here now or ever. That said, it is time to let the healing process begin. Dominic Winters and his creation are gone from our lives, so let us lower our fists, soften our words, and be a community once more."

Mr. Miller and several dozens of his previously incensed community members attended Dom's funeral, maintaining a respectful gap between themselves and the friends, family and art school faculty who lovingly encircled Dom's casket. It was a well-attended but otherwise simple, quiet ceremony featuring a few of Dom's strongest pieces.

Evan Johns was tired to the core. Like most of the department, it would take awhile for his emotions to sort themselves out. He had put that task off to some degree by overseeing the design and construction of the Winters Building, and tonight, as he rolled up a set of structural drawings and signed off on a couple of the remaining touches, he began to feel the weight of Dom's absence. Johns ran his hand over the package in his breast pocket and felt his heart ache. He took a deep breath and shook the feeling from his head before it got the better of him, then put on his coat and turned off the studio lights.

What the freshly-erected Winters building lacks in magnitude, it makes up for in grace and ingenuity, a product of the combined minds, hearts and hands of the graduate students and professors who knew Dom best. Its entryway is a peculiar combination of stark utilitarianism and elegant warmth, a tribute to Dom's more marketable qualities. The heart of the structure lies just inside: its atrium. Scattered polygonal skylights that are almost unnoticeable from the front of the building overlook a less organic lattice of stainless steel and black marble. The steel girders turn to form the bridges between the four glass doors that have only frosted rectangular pads in place of handles. The floor is composed of tiles in varying shapes and shades of white marble, forming concentric arcs that revolve about the atrium's centerpiece, an abstract relief sculpture of ornately carved birch surrounding a rectangular window that covers a small, stark, and currently empty chamber.

Alex and Karen were waiting here for the professor. He smiled at them and said, "Hi guys." The three converged on the center display, where Johns inserted a key into an inconspicuously-placed lock beneath the glass window, exposing the empty chamber. Aside from white plaster, the chamber contained only the butt end of a single brass nail. Johns unbuttoned his pocket and pulled out a yellow envelope, which he held out for Alex. "This is your job."

Alex reached out and took the package, stared at it for a moment, then removed its contents: a small teak square with a torn piece of sketch paper sealed onto it by a crystal plate. He looked up at Evan and Karen through teary eyes, then back down at the placard in his hand.

"You were too big for your chair, Dom," he said. "You... were your own greatest work of art." Karen was crying into her hands but wiping the tears from her eyes, not wanting to miss the moment. Johns was more stoically allowing tears to fall. "I hope that everyone who passes through this room comes to understand what you went through... and..." A tear fell from Alex's nose toward the placard and he pulled it away just in time. "And why."

He took a deep breath before stepping forward and raising the placard to the wall. Carefully he hung and straightened it, then closed the door. The trio lingered for several moments trying to get their sadness under control.

Johns took a last look at the wall and said quietly, "Who wants a drink?"

Karen smiled through red eyes and almost whispered, "I do."

Alex nodded. Johns reached over and flipped a pair of switches on the wall as they walked out into the chilly winter night. All the lights in the atrium died except for a single, down-facing sconce illuminating a solitary piece of paper. It said:

untitled,
Dominic Winters

about the author

J. Whitfield Gurley is an artist and designer in Portland, Oregon. When he's not writing about himself in the third person, he enjoys creating in other mediums: music, sculpture, drawing and painting. He lives with his lovely wife Suzanne and an elderly cat and dog that will likely be a totally different cat and dog by the time you finish reading this sentence.

CPSIA information can be obtained
at www.ICGtesting.com
Printed in the USA
LVHW080834100121
675636LV00008B/792